Enjoy the trip to

MW00335568

Cheryl &om

Maddy°

Lori Piotrowski

i

Revolutionary Spirit

Books in The Molly Weston Chronicles

Revolutionary Heart
Revolutionary Spirit

Revolutionary Spirit

The Molly Weston Chronicles

Lori Piotrowski

February Productions

February Productions
3870 E. Flamingo Rd., Ste. A2PMB 542
Las Vegas, NV 89121

Cover art by Custom Book Teasers artist Rachael Tamayo
rtamayo2004@gmail.com

Thank you for purchasing this copy of *Revolutionary Spirit*. If you enjoyed reading it, please consider purchasing additional copies for your friends and loved ones to read. Thank you for respecting the hours put into creating this work of fiction for your pleasure.

Printed in the United States of America

ISBN: 978-1-7324048-2-3

A Note to My Readers

Writing is a solitary adventure, but eventually an author needs extra eyes. For *Revolutionary Spirit,* two friends stepped forward to help me proof: Cindy Oyler-Pape and Karen Lampus. Your assistance is invaluable.

For my readers, thanks for reading *Revolutionary Spirit.* I invite you to visit my web site (www.loripiotrowski.com) for information about my books, research nuggets, and information about book signings and upcoming releases. While there, sign up for my newsletter that will keep you informed about the Patriots. Also, please consider writing a review to help me and other readers!

Visit the author's website at www.loripiotrowski.com
Sign up for the author's newsletter at www.loripiotrowski.com

For the men in my life
James, Russ, Rich, Peter, and JP

Table of Contents

Prologue   1

November 1765   2

Eli Weston   2

Geoffrey Canfield   4

Molly Weston   6

December 1765   8

Eli Weston   8

Molly Weston   10

May 1766   14

Geoffrey Canfield   14

Molly Weston   18

Eli Weston   24

Molly Weston   26

June 1766   31

Eli Weston   31

Molly Weston   34

Geoffrey Canfield   38

July 1766   40

Molly Weston   40

Geoffrey Canfield   42

Molly Weston   44

August 1766   49

Eli Weston   49

Geoffrey Canfield   51

Molly Weston   54

September 1766   56

Molly Weston   56

Eli Weston   58

Geoffrey Canfield   59

Eli Weston   61

Geoffrey Canfield   63

October 1766   66

Molly Weston   66

Geoffrey Canfield   68

Hester Winslow   70

Geoffrey Canfield   72

Eli Weston   74

November 1766   77

Molly Weston   77

January 1767   79

Hester Winslow   79

Geoffrey Canfield   82

Hester Winslow   84

February 1767   86

Eli Weston   86

April 1767   89

Hester Winslow   89

May 1767   91

Molly Weston   91

June 1767   93

    Eli Weston   93

    Molly Weston   95

July 1767   98

    Eli Weston   98

August 1767   100

    Molly Weston   100

    Geoffrey Canfield   102

    Eli Weston   104

    Geoffrey Canfield   108

    Eli Weston   111

September 1767   114

    Eli Weston   114

    Geoffrey Canfield   119

    Eli Weston   122

    Geoffrey Canfield   124

October 1767   127

    Molly Weston   127

    Eli Weston   134

    Geoffrey Canfield   137

    Eli Weston   139

    Molly Weston   143

    Hester Winslow   150

November 1767   153

    Geoffrey Canfield   153

    Eli Weston   155

Geoffrey Canfield   *157*

Molly Weston   *159*

Eli Weston   *161*

Molly Weston   *167*

December 1767   **173**

Geoffrey Canfield   *173*

Molly Weston   *175*

Hester Winslow   *178*

Molly Weston   *180*

January 1768   **183**

Molly Weston   *183*

Geoffrey Canfield   *186*

Eli Weston   *189*

Henry Weston   *192*

February 1768   **195**

Molly Weston   *195*

Addenda   **200**

Holiday Cooky   *201*

Currency Act of 1764   *203*

Declaratory Act of 1766   *205*

An Inquiry Into the Rights of the British Colonies   *207*

The Townshend Revenue Act   *213*

References   *217*

The People, even to the lowest Ranks, have become more attentive to their Liberties, more inquisitive about them, and more determined to defend them, than they were ever before known or had occasion to be.

— *From the diary of John Adams, December 18, 1765*

Prologue

I gaze into my beloved's eyes and, in the depth of those blue irises, tiny gold and green flecks glow with warmth. We are so close that I can feel his breath fall across my face, and I can focus on only one eye at a time. I smile thinking how my eyes, flitting from one of his to the other, must appear jumpy to him.

We are waiting a response. My anticipation of disapproval grows. We have gone through many trials, and we have made many enemies. Others have the right to be angry.

Yet we are here, holding one another's hands, anticipating our future, and waiting. The muffled sounds of infants and scuffling shoes grow faint as I fall into my memory's abyss . . .

November 1765

Eli Weston

Fire rained down upon us. The night sky hailed a barrage of stones and chunks of mortar. Thundering beams shot from the mill and pierced the darkness like arrows as they flew toward their human targets.

"Hurry! Before the powder catches fire!"

Lt. Canfield and Jack did a three-legged hobble half-carrying, half-dragging the sailor's companion toward the trees where they collapsed to the ground. Finally, my own legs gave out, and I dumped Jack's henchman off my back and toppled to the ground. The air was hot and ashy; I covered my mouth and nose with my checkered scarf to protect my lungs, yet still I hacked as the thick smoke penetrated the fabric.

The fire crackled and when a log broke with a loud snap, I jumped back into the kitchen of The Three Lions. After the mill's explosion, our group had retreated to my father's tavern in Boston to eat and drink and replenish our spirits. A few of the men had chuckled nervously upon hearing the log break. It was too soon after the mill explosion for us to sit peaceably next to a fire, even though this one was of a friendly nature.

Mother daubed scratches and bruises with her ointments and applied poultices to the severest injuries. An occasional yelp escaped from the men's maws as she scrubbed a cut too vigorously or wound a bandage too tightly. She grimaced, her lips taut as a bowline as she treated our wounds. The tenderest touch she reserved for my sister Molly, who had suffered the most.

"Molly . . . Molly," she softly called to her daughter.

"Mother, let her be," I said. "She'll come 'round in time."

"Eli, 'tis possible, but she could withdraw even more. What happened at the mill? Why has she been injured?"

Although she had been wrapped in blankets and placed closest to the fire for warmth, Molly shivered uncontrollably. She had been in bonds for so long that the hemp had scraped off layers of skin. Dark purple rings circled her wrists and the bruising leached up her forearms. As mother cleansed the wounds, they opened up again and drops of blood seeped through the scabbed tissue. In later years, unsightly scars, white bracelets on each hand, would remind her every day of the horrors she had endured.

"Jack kept her tied. The rope ate into her skin as she worked herself free."

Mother's eyes teared up, and she rubbed her hands over her face to compose herself.

"We didn't know she was there . . . in the barn . . . that is, Geoffrey knew, but couldn't reach her once Jack started the fight. Molly was on her own."

My sister's wrists would heal, as would the scrapes on her cheek and forehead. It was her spirit that concerned me. Would she ever be the carefree and headstrong girl who tagged along behind me? Or would her ordeal forever silence her and sentence her to a life of quiet servitude? I sighed and wished she could give me a sign of which road to healing she would take.

Geoffrey Canfield

Jackrabbits couldn't have run faster than when Eli, Jack, and I saw the lantern's flames dance across the dry timber in the mill. And as the mill exploded, we were already racing to outrun its fiery debris. After Jack and I dumped his thuggish cohort on the ground, I turned my attention to my beloved.

"Molly! Molly!"

I scanned the area to find her, but it was Matthew's body I espied first. He had been felled by a piece of mill shrapnel. As I looked up from the ground, I saw that Eli's good friend, Cotton, had found his way to Molly and loosed her bonds. As I drew near, I could see her fall and Cotton leaning over her. Something in his demeanor made me pause.

To my surprise, she wrapped her arms around him and he her. What sort of chicanery was this? Molly and I had an understanding. At least, I thought we did.

Cotton carried Molly and placed her gently on the wagon seat before climbing up beside her. He was talking to her, but the distance prevented me from understanding. I watched as he draped several blankets gleaned from the tents over her shoulders. She leaned into his body and he placed his arm around her in a protective gesture. Her head lolled against his shoulder.

Not wanting to dwell on the outlandish affection being shown between the two, I busied myself looking for the rest of our men. Eli and I gathered them up and we loaded the remaining wagon with the wounded. Those who could still ride found horses that had fled the barn, or commandeered those who no longer had owners, and we formed a raggedy parade back to the city.

"Come in, come in!" Elizabeth Weston, mother to Eli and Molly, welcomed us into The Three Lions' kitchen despite the morning's early hour.

"Paul! Pour some ale. Henry! Give these men a trencher of stew," she ordered her sons about. She then turned to me. "Get my sickness kit from the shelf. Now!"

As more men poured into the tavern, Eli's younger brothers Paul and Henry began to serve up bowls of stew with remnants of yesterday's bread, already turning hard and crusty. Nobody minded the staleness as we all inhaled the nourishment. As our bellies filled, our bodies warmed, and all the while Elizabeth moved from man to man with her medicinal ministrations.

From time to time, I carefully eyed Molly. My love had retreated into her mind, and her body shook. Vacant eyes stared into nothingness, and I wondered where she was and what she was thinking. Perhaps I had misjudged Cotton's actions, but I vowed to watch him closely. His intimate actions toward Molly demanded my resolute attention.

Molly Weston

The events of that first week of November were not to be forgotten. Over and over again, I felt more than I saw Jack wrapping my hands with rope and leading me from an abandoned building in Boston followed by a long wagon ride to a mill and then out to a barn where he tethered me to a support beam. Those British sailors who were helping Captain Willson and General Bridgewater steal sulphur to make, and then hoard, black powder, had brought me to where they were storing their illegal munitions. If only I had been able to espy my brother Eli or Geoffrey before the demons had unleashed their fiery maelstrom.

Instead, I was accosted by Matthew, who had once served Lt. Gov. Thomas Hutchinson at Castle William and was loyal to the same. My escape served only to provide him with a hostage, and fulfilling his duties, he had tied me to a tree along the edge of the clearing. A position that gave me a clear view of the looming disaster.

And so, I watched, unable to render assistance, unable to prevent what I could foresee. Two blasts shattered the night: The first was the mill and the second was the barn I had escaped only a few minutes earlier. Horses and men screamed and ran, animals and humans hoping to escape the inferno that attacked from two sides. The successive force from the blasts punched my body, shoving my right cheek into the rough tree bark. The heat scorched my bared face and hands; I pinched my eyes shut in an effort to preserve my sight.

Suddenly, all was quiet. And then through the darkness, I heard someone calling my name. My arms flew back as the bonds were cut and the momentum propelled me away from the tree and onto my back. The ground was hard and cold; the air hot from the blazing mill. I opened my eyes to see Matthew lying on the ground an arm's length away and my brother's good friend leaning over me.

"Oh, Cotton!" I wept for joy and reached for his arms.

Relief was the first emotion to wash over me; the second was exhaustion. My weakened disposition allowed Cotton to assume control of the situation, and he quickly carried me to a wagon and gently placed me into the seat before climbing up beside me.

I could hear him say something, but his voice was so far away. When he wrapped his arm around my shoulders, the invitation to give in to my fatigue overcame my sense of propriety. The warmth of his body comforted me, and I remembered only a sense of peace and safety encircling my soul as I drifted off.

For several days after the explosion, I rested, knowing that soon I would need to return to Anna's shop and my job. But every time I opened the kitchen door to the alley, my hands began to shake and soon my whole body would shiver as I relived my kidnapping. Both mother and father urged me to rest, but I knew I had to rid myself of the fear.

After a week, my pride shook me awake and I vowed to conquer my anxiety. With our dog Boots by my side, I bundled up and set out for a walk to do some shopping. I shivered from the cold and nerves. As I walked, however, I found that my body warmed and I could feel the tight grasp of fear loosen as friends and acquaintances nodded and greeted me along the way.

December 1765

Eli Weston

Cotton smiled at the memory and began to tell his story.

"No, it wasn't difficult to avoid the sailors. I tracked them like we did when we'd hunt deer, Eli. Except that it was much easier because they didn't know enough to not leave a trail as wide as a pair of yoked oxen."

I laughed aloud, perhaps too boisterously, but mostly out of relief to have my friend back by my side. We had managed to get back into Boston, but Cotton had disappeared no sooner had he carried my sister into The Three Lions. Now, several weeks later, he had stopped by. He said it was to talk to me and Geoffrey, but there was an air about him that made me believe there was another reason — Molly. Oddly enough, Geoffrey had made himself scarce after our return from the mill. Obviously, he came and went — he was billeted at the tavern after all — but his rosy nature had sprouted a few thorns.

"But how did they manage to capture you?" interrupted my sister. I could see that she was still not convinced of what she perceived as Cotton's change of heart. She had thought him a traitor as she watched him and Matthew at the mill.

"That, I have to say, was a stroke of genius," he continued. Molly stared at him incredulously.

"Tracking gives a fellow plenty of time to think, and I began to wonder whether I could make their heads spin. So, I decided to let them catch me. With Geoffrey heading over to Castle Island the next week, I didn't figure I'd be held all that long. What I didn't count on, though, was such an easy escape from Castle William. That Matthew, now he was quite the jailer!" He laughed, but it lacked mirth.

"Your faith in us is admirable," said Geoffrey. "I daresay that it's much stronger than that which I may have had in you." The lieutenant's toneless comment startled me; evidently, he had sneaked in while we were gripped by the adventuresome tale, leaned against the door jamb, and crossed his arms. When I took in his expression and his stance, he looked more a warrior than a friend.

I put my arm around the lieutenant's shoulders and patted his back to ease him back into a sense of comradery.

"But it worked!" Cotton continued. "The worst part was sitting in the basement of Castle William for a week waiting for you and Matthew to work out details of my escape. At least they fed me well!"

He smiled and winked at Molly. Geoffrey stiffened even more at seeing that small gesture of familiarity.

To her credit, Molly rolled her eyes and turned back to the hearth where she was tending a gobbet stew, seemingly oblivious to the crowing of one potential suitor and the glowering of another.

At this mention of Matthew, however, a somber mood descended upon us all. No one yet dared to speak what we all knew to be true about the Lt. Governor's manservant. We had been betrayed by someone we had taken into our confidence. Matthew lost his life because he served Thomas Hutchison. And because of his death, we learned that what we had deemed previously to be a tenuous connection between Lt. Governor Hutchison and General Bridgewater was in truth a strong bond.

What we had yet to learn, however, was whether Matthew had revealed the depth of Geoffrey's betrayal to the Crown. My British friend's activities on our behalf could lead him to swing from the gibbet for his treasonous crimes.

Molly Weston

We were relieved to learn that Cotton was not a British spy, although I had sensed that was true from the moment he had loosed me from that tree. From the depth of my being I knew that he would never betray us. I was shamed whenever I thought back on the moments of my captivity that had caused me to question what my heart knew to be true. It felt good to hear him laugh with Eli and the others, yet nobody had raised the question of Matthew and the part he had played in their plan. A plan that Geoffrey had concocted with the British loyalist. A plan that threw Cotton together with that same man who had worked for the lieutenant governor. Was it possible that both Cotton and Geoffrey could have been so easily fooled by one man?

The men paused for a moment at the mention of Matthew, but then carried on as if Hutchinson's servant hadn't existed. Certainly, he didn't exist for them now. But they hadn't seen his face when he attacked me. They didn't know the level of his betrayal. If the mill hadn't exploded at that moment . . . I shuddered and shook my head to clear the vision. But before I could erase it, my stomach clenched and the memories came at me in a torrent. I clutched at the mantel to keep from doubling over. I wouldn't continue thinking this way . . . I couldn't! The horror of that night was over. I needed to breathe and maintain control. I needed to look forward and keep my eyes on the future.

♥

It wasn't but a fortnight before impending tragedy loomed once more. My kidnapper, Jack, had been suffering from the pox when he abducted me. The two days I spent near him had given rise to a fever in my body. Mother sent me to bed and watched closely. My fever abated rather quickly, and fortunately, the pustules that could leave one pockmarked for life never formed on me. I had escaped the wrath of that dreadful disease, which instead visited Eli who fell ill several days after my fever struck.

Eli had returned from the docks that evening complaining of work as he often did. He stretched to ease his aching back, but soon began grumbling about his head. Mother was quick to send him to bed. When I brought him a tray for supper, I saw that his face had paled and he waived off the food.

"Let me check you for fever, Eli."

He mumbled an unintelligible reply, so I moved forward. His head jerked backward as I placed my cool hand on his burning cheek, and I knew the disease had afflicted him. Boston had experienced an epidemic in 1721; grandfather often spoke of the hundreds of persons who had perished from the pox. I pushed down thoughts of my brother dying and vowed to bring him back to health.

Over the next couple of days, high fever left his bedclothes wet from perspiration. As rapidly as he drenched them, I carried them to the kitchen to boil them clean and hang them by the fire to dry. However, once his rash began to ooze puss, father closed The Three Lions in a self-imposed quarantine. Mother observed strict protocols regarding illness, and she allowed only Geoffrey and me near him. Because my fever had been a mild case, I was left immune to the disease. Geoffrey's family, like many in Britain, had been exposed to the dreaded pox when he was a child. He and his brother survived while so many in the greater London area had not.

Small, roundish pustules dotted Eli's legs, torso, arms, neck, and face so thickly that barely an inch was left smooth. I watched my dearest brother struggle with the disease and I tried to ease his discomfort. I sat by his bed and ministered to him as I had learned from watching mother. Her supply of willow bark, steeped in boiling water, gave me a tincture to ease his pain. Some I made him drink and some I used to soak small rags that I used to bathe his sores.

When I wasn't nursing him, I read to him, sharing some of the latest articles from the *Gazette*.

Geoffrey and I took turns caring for him, spelling one another when fatigue took root in our bones. After an exhaustive week, Eli's fever subsided, and by the end of the second week, his sores had scabbed over. It was another week, however, before the scabs fell off and we could see how the pox had ravaged his face. The face of a twenty-four-year old, craggy and creviced as that of an old man, looked back at us. His smile hadn't returned, and the sparkle in his eyes had yet to catch light, but he was whole. And he was with us.

✦

We Westons typically didn't celebrate Christmas other than to attend services at West Church, but this year was an exception. There was so much to give thanks for: the defeat of Bridgewater-Willson's gang, the destruction of their cache of black powder, Eli's health. Mother and I wanted to make a special meal; my contribution would be to make a Christmas cooky.

On December 24th, I set about gathering my ingredients: flour, sugar, milk, butter, and sugar. I spooned out a good portion of coriander seeds that would flavor the buttery shortbread and ground them to a fine powder. And because this was to be a special occasion, I also ground some cinnamon and nutmeg to add to the chocolate that I would melt and drizzle on top of the baked confections. More than anything, I wanted tomorrow to create a good memory for all of us.

The cookies were baked and cooling, their sweet aroma filling the kitchen, and I had begun melting the chocolate when Geoffrey walked in. This last step required much attention for should the pot became too hot, the chocolate would burn and its texture become crumbly. I stirred the thick mixture, twirling my spoon from left to right and round and round, all the while moving the pot closer to and further away from the fire as needed to maintain a constant temperature. I was aware of his presence, but my attention needed to be on completing this finishing touch.

Once the chocolate was smooth and of a velvety consistency, I dipped the back of a small spoon into the chocolate and drizzled it over a cooky. I offered it to Geoffrey.

"Taste."

He hesitated, then pinched it between his finger and thumb and bit into the shortbread.

"Mmm." He looked at me appraisingly, then nodded and chewed the last morsel.

"They're for tomorrow. You'll be joining us for Christmas dinner, won't you?" His behavior toward me the last month had cooled, and I hoped the invitation would warm his disposition.

"We are patrolling tomorrow. It would be best to not plan on me."

I watched him leave, and a bit of my heart followed him. His change of demeanor confused me. Our being seen in public had started as a ruse for us to get closer to those who could direct us to Bridgewater's cache of black powder. We hadn't expected to develop feelings for one another, but we did. We had talked of a future together. We had kissed. Stinging tears sprung to my eyes, but I wouldn't let them fall. I wouldn't let any man make a fool of me.

May 1766

Geoffrey Canfield

From time to time, Jack's face would come to mind, and I marveled at how someone suffering from the pox could have devised and carried out such a devious kidnapping plan. That he could even stand amazed me, but then I had seen men in battle perform under even more adverse circumstances. Most of Eli's care, however, fell to Molly, who had escaped the most virulent form of the pox, and me to care for him. Molly would not leave Eli's room until I returned from patrol. I spelled her as long as I could, leaving myself only a few hours of sleep each night.

Jonathan Weston closed the tavern at the first visible sign of the contagion in an effort to avoid spreading the disease throughout the city. The family and we three boarders closed ranks to wait out the illness. My soldiers and I were immune to the disease, having been exposed to it on British soil, and when Eli was stricken, we were free to continue our patrols.

It was imperative that I continue to be seen by my troops as well as by my superiors. We had succeeded in destroying General Bridgewater's cache of black powder, but in doing so, we had left ourselves no means to prove that he and Captain Willson had been manufacturing munitions. What we had succeeded in doing was to leave ourselves and our future actions open to scrutiny and investigation. My only path to survival in the Royal Army in Boston was to parry that interest elsewhere. And that required finding something that would pique the general's interest. And that would take some time.

It wasn't until May that a letter from my father, the Earl of Eastleigh, brought troubling news. Dated March 18, he wrote that during the last session of Parliament, several members had sought to repeal the Stamp Act citing the riotous reaction in the colonies. The vote to repeal had passed, but father warned me that the colonists would still be taxed. Parliament was determined to raise monies to offset its war debt.

"It would behoove you to convey the importance of taxes to support His Majesty," my father wrote. "Great Britain has been generous in its defense of the colonies, and until now, has overlooked many infractions of the tax laws. One must participate in one's defense, and soldiering is but one of the ways to participate. The second, and more common way, is to share the financial burden of such a necessary defense."

After several paragraphs explaining how I was to frame the argument, he concluded, "Exchequer Townshend is a strong proponent of taxation. It would be wise to help ensure the colonists consent to a tax in some form."

I unfolded a torn piece of newspaper on which my father had circled a small article hailing from Westminster.

> This day his Majesty came to the house of Peers, and being in his royal robes, seated on the throne, with the usual solemnity, Sir *Francis Molineux,* Gentleman usher of the black rod was sent with a Message from his Majesty to the house of commons, commanding their attendance in the house of peers. The commons being come thither accordingly, his Majesty was pleased to give his Royal Assent to
> An ACT to *Repeal an Act,* made the last Session of Parliament, entitled, An Act for granting and applying duties, and other duties in the *British* Colonies and Plantations in *America,* towards further defraying the Expences of defending, protecting, and securing the same . . .[1]

I sat at my make-shift desk and pondered the implications. News that the Stamp Act had been repealed would be received happily by all I knew. Yet my father's insistence that American colonists must acquiesce to taxes and his tone when mentioning the new exchequer of the treasury did not sit well in my mind, and for good reason. Within a week, all the Boston newspapers would publish The Declaratory Act:

> March 18, 1766
> AN ACT for the better securing the dependency of his Majesty's dominions in America upon the crown and parliament of Great Britain . . .
>
> That the said colonies and plantations in *America* have been, are, and of right ought to be subordinate unto, and dependent upon the imperial crown and parliament of *Great Britain*; and that the King's majesty, by and with the advice and consent of the lords spiritual and temporal, and commons of *Great Britain*, in parliament assembled, had, hath, and of right ought to have, full power and authority to make laws and statutes of sufficient force and validity to bind the colonies and people of *America*, subjects of the crown of *Great Britain*, in all cases whatsoever.
>
> II. And be it further declared . . . That all resolutions, votes, orders, and proceedings, in any of the said colonies or plantations, whereby the power and

[1] *London Gazette*, March 18, 1766.

authority of the parliament of *Great Britain*, to make laws and statutes as aforesaid, is denied, or drawn into question, are, and are hereby declared to be, utterly null and void to all intents and purposes whatsoever.[2]

Parliament was indeed working against the colonies. The first line declaring Parliament's goal to retain tight control over its colonies was troublesome. But it was that last line, "in all cases whatsoever," that would run through my head day after day. Like a church bell sounding a death knell, I could hear "in all cases, in all cases." Parliament had succinctly outlined its power over the British colonies in three words. My mind endeavored to buoy my hopes that with the Stamp Act repealed all hostilities between the two continents would evaporate. My military education as well as my soldiering instincts, however, were leading my thoughts in the opposite direction.

---

[2] Retrieved May 31, 2016 from http://www.stamp-act-history.com/documents/1766-declaratory-act-original-text

Molly Weston

May was turning out to be a lovely month. The last of the snow had melted and spring blossoms were everywhere. The magnolia trees had finally come into full bloom, their deep pink petals as big as my hand. Gardens along the Common had sprouted beds of glowing white narcissus and brilliant pink azaleas. In a few days, the heady scent of hundreds of lilac bushes would waft through the streets.

But it wasn't only the flowers that raised my spirits. Boston was all a-chatter with the news. The Stamp Act had been repealed! I practically danced along Queene Street from Mr. Edes' office after leaving him with my latest advice for publication. Finally, he had published the wonderful news that everyone had been whispering about for several days. Everywhere I went that day people were talking about the success of our boycott. The *Gazette* even mentioned that the King was pleased with the repeal and even the townspeople in London were joyful at hearing the news.

Our efforts had convinced Parliament of the righteousness of our stance on excessive taxation, and now, the entire city was getting ready to celebrate on Friday. John Hancock had posted bills around the city declaring his house and others along Boston Common to be open in the afternoon and evening for refreshments so the city could revel in our good fortune. Preparations were being made for a firework display in the Common that evening. The sun had vanquished the dark night and everyone had arisen to the brightness of a new day.

I was hopeful, too, that the evening's festivities would help to lessen the tension between Geoffrey and me. Last year, Geoffrey and I had forged a bond, but somehow my kidnapping and the mill explosion had broken it. Now, Eli had managed that the three of us would attend together. I sighed, thinking back to the magical night of

18

the electricity demonstration last August. That evening had given me such hope for my future. But now . . .

I don't know why I keep thinking about Geoffrey. When I think of how aloof he has been, and with Cotton had been stopping by more frequently, I'm inclined to favor my brother's friend. After all, even I can see that Cotton isn't stopping in just to talk to Eli. He spends as much time with me. My heart, however, still struggles with memories of my British lieutenant.

♥

Music had been playing all morning long, and at one o'clock, the Castle and all the batteries were fired, giving the Royal Salute. The crowd cheered at hearing the cannons roar, and then turned to even more singing and dancing in the streets. The exuberance of the celebration, however, had not yet found its way to my second-floor room.

Mother sat on the bed as I pondered the ribbons that would accent my dress. I had planned on wearing my lavender silk dress, and normally I would have reached for the strands of purple satin to lace the stomacher, but tonight I was hesitant to wear the same attire as the night of the electricity experiment. That night had changed my feelings toward Geoffrey, and wearing the same dress was bringing back all those memories. His aloofness had made me begin to question whether we really had fallen in love. It had been so thrilling to work alongside him to bring down the Bridgewater-Willson gang. Our late-night conversations, brief kisses in the kitchen . . .

"You seem lost in thought, dear," she said.

"Oh, mother! I don't know what's gotten into Geoffrey, what's gotten into me! All was going so well. I know our outings began as a pretense to be seen in public as a couple and learn what Bridgewater was doing, but our relationship developed further. And now he avoids me. Did I really imagine that he liked me? We talked for hours about his dreams for a farm. He seemed so genuine when we were together, and now nothing. And I can't stop thinking about him."

I sighed and ran the ribbons through my fingers.
"Well, at least Cotton speaks to me."

"Don't be so petulant, child! Have you no idea as to why Geoffrey has avoided you? My goodness, but you must be daft! Have you no recall of what happened after the explosion?"

My heart fluttered for a moment as a seed of fear entered into my being.

"Your face tells me you don't, so perhaps I can help. According to Eli, it was Cotton who cut the ropes from your wrists."

"Of course, it was! I know that." My eyes fell to the still pink scars, brands from the hemp that had bound me.

"Men feel differently about things than we do, Molly. It's likely that Geoffrey believes that Cotton has wormed his way in between you two. In his mind, he should have been the one to rescue you and consequently care for you."

"Oh, no!" I sighed and fell on the bed next to her. However, would I get through the night knowing that I was the one who had driven Geoffrey away.

✦

That evening, as Eli, Geoffrey, and I strolled along Mount Street, the lieutenant was especially quiet. Quiet in that he wasn't speaking, which suited my mood, but his energy spoke otherwise. His walking pace was sporadic, his stride lengthening until it seemed that even Eli had trouble in keeping up before he would slow. At one point, when he was several yards ahead, he abruptly stopped and turned to face us.

"This celebration isn't warranted," he began. "We should be spending our time in consultation rather than exultation."

"Geoffrey, whatever are you talking about?" Eli asked. His tone worried me and I looked at the two men whose faces were gloomier than the day's festivities warranted.

"My father has sent word in his last letter. The Stamp Act was repealed, yes, but Parliament, in his judgment, and in mine, has put in its place something more extreme. You've seen it in the *Gazette*, but for now know that this latest legislation, the Declaratory Act, has the potential to quash America. This act is only the beginning of legislation Parliament is planning that will be more destructive to the colonies."

"What?" I couldn't believe what he was saying. Tonight, we were to celebrate our freedom from that onerous stamp tax. Certainly, he is mistaken.

Although the sun was setting, the world now seemed much darker than a few moments before. Suddenly I felt like crying. All the pent-up emotions I felt at Jack and Salmon kidnapping me, the horror at seeing Matthew killed in front of me, and the fear of my own imminent death as the mill exploded came pouring out of me.

"No! It can't be! We worked so hard to make them listen! It . . . it can't be . . ."

Eli recognized my anguish and reached out to pull me to his breast. I felt comforted by my brother's embrace, but my mind said that Geoffrey should have been the one to reach out to hold me. Knowing that it was my fault that Geoffrey no longer searched me out in the kitchen, that he now sought out excuses to leave a room whenever I entered, tore at my heart. The moment we had demolished the mill and fractured General Bridgewater's gang, our relationship too had shattered. Thinking of the love that had been lost made me want to sob, and at this moment, more than anything I wanted to feel my Geoffrey's arms around me, my brother's strong arms would have to do.

However, my sense of decorum and dignity prevented me from turning into a young schoolgirl. I fought back the tears and forced myself to breathe deeply. Once the burning in my eyes, cheeks, and nose had calmed, I pushed back from Eli's arms.

The Stamp Act repeal had boosted the spirits of Bostonians. It was difficult to remain sad amid so much revelry, so I swallowed my emotions and we three continued our way to the Common.

For several days, the Sons of Liberty had been building a tall pyramid near Liberty Tree. Now that we had reached the Common, we could see the enormous structure. The upper four stories were decorated with statues of the King and Queen and 14 colonists who had worked so hard on the repeal. I recognized Samuel Adams and James Otis in miniature, but then had to laugh out loud when I realized that most of the statues bore the same faces. Atop the pyramid sat a circular platform lined with fireworks.[3]

From house to house, we reveled. Laughter and gaiety surrounded us as we made our way around the Common. Cattle had been corralled at one end of the space for the day and the remainder of the grassy expanse was thick with people greeting one another with handshakes and embraces, kisses and toasts. We made our way to the Hancock house on Beacon Street, where the lawyer had erected his own stage for fireworks and set up an enormous cask in the front garden that was dispensing Madeira wine to any who had a glass to fill. In single file, we finally managed to climb the front stairs and squeeze into the front room.

Toward the unlit fireplace we found the lawyer talking with other Sons of Liberty, including Dr. Warren and William Molineux,

---

[3] *Boston-Gazette, and Country Journal,* May 26, 1766.

one of the city's merchants who spent as much time on the docks as in his warehouse. Hailing from Albany, New York, Dr. Thomas Young, had recently joined the Sons of Liberty as well as the North End Caucus. Their closed circle and whispers were at odds with the revelry that surrounded them. Drs. Warren and Young and Mr. Molineux stepped back as Mr. Hancock moved forward, his smiling face carrying a welcome greeting.

"Eli, Geoffrey, and Miss Molly. Come join us in a celebratory drink. The punch, I assure you, Molly, is most suitable for young ladies."

He took me by the arm and escorted me through the front room and into the ballroom where many of the ladies were grouped together in cheery conversation.

"Mercy Warren, may I introduce Molly Weston. Molly, you will recognize Mercy as the younger and more beautiful of the Otis family."

"John, such wit becomes you! Molly, come join us while the men discuss the problems of the world. By the way they cloister themselves in conversation, one would never know that today was to be a celebration." She winked at John and took my arm in hers.

A loud boom startled all of us, and after a moment's pause, we began to laugh. The fireworks had begun.

Eli Weston

Cotton had decided to remove himself from the docks after the Bridgewater-Willson affair, and he had persuaded Paul to work alongside him in the forests logging. Paul, for his part, was more than happy to leave The Three Lions and earn a living on his own. The British Royal Navy had been searching out trees in the white pine forests of the Bay and New Hampshire colonies and marking them with the King's broad arrow — a vertical hatchet mark with an outward slanted mark on either side to form an arrowhead shape.

Trees with such a mark were to be harvested and shipped to Britain. White pine was ideal for marine uses— it was lightweight and strong. A mast for the best sailing ships could soar 90 feet, and the British needed such masts to maintain their fleet of men-of-war. Our forests grew the best trees, tall trees, very tall and straight trees.[4] Cotton and Paul joined a small army of men who would spend the week at a camp and return to the city on Saturday afternoons.

"I cannot believe it! The Stamp Act repealed!" Cotton laughed heartily at the news while scanning the tavern's great room. Looking for Molly again.

"Stay in town this week. Big celebrations taking place on Friday. And a ball on Friday next."

Cotton slaked his thirst and rose from the table.

"Perhaps I will."

---

[4] "The King's Broad Arrow and Eastern White Pine," Northeastern Lumber Manufacturers Association, http://www.nelma.org. Retrieved June 28, 2017.

He headed toward the kitchen, undoubtedly looking for my sister. Paul looked at me with a question in his eyes, and I could only shrug.

"None of your business. Nor mine."

Molly Weston

"Molly! Molly!"

I turned at hearing my name and found myself nose-to-chest with Cotton. His big smile greeted me warmly and I couldn't help but giggle. He was my big brother's best friend and, at times, I still felt like a smitten young girl whenever he was near.

"May I escort you to the ball Friday next?"

"A ball? I had no idea you could dance. Who is holding such an extravagant affair?"

"I don't know, but I do know that I would be honored to have you on my arm that evening."

"Cotton! Such foolishness! You request my attendance at a ball for which you have no invitation? What kind of offer is that?"

"A sincere one, Molly. Please?"

Who could resist those soft brown eyes? This attention was more than I had received from Geoffrey in several months. I smiled and nodded my reply.

"But only if you have a bona fide invitation."

I watched him head back into the great room and began to busy myself once again with the dough for supper's pasties.

Attending a gala could be an enjoyable evening. Definitely an unforgettable event. My lavender petticoat and purple ribbons would be sufficient dress for the occasion. But that petticoat again! Memories of attending the electricity demonstration with Geoffrey rushed into view once more. Again, I felt his strength as he clasped my hand to help me to the stage and I envisioned his face filled with attentive concern for my well-being. He was a gentleman and a perfect escort.

A sigh escaped my lips before I could catch it. I shook my head to clear the daydream. Geoffrey wouldn't be asking me to attend. It would be best to focus on supper.

Cotton was true to his word. Within two days, he had secured an invitation to the celebratory ball and sent word that he would collect me at eight o'clock on Friday evening. As the time drew nearer, I found myself hoping I could find an excuse to not attend the gala. I liked Cotton, but I didn't *like* Cotton. And to put a crown on my teetertottering emotions, I had but one petticoat for dress. Once again, I donned that lavender petticoat and concentrated on not thinking about a certain British officer. Mother came up to help me arrange my hair and then fussed about the room as I tried to collect myself.

"Have your feelings changed toward Cotton?" she asked.

"Oh, mother! Of course not! But Cotton invited me; Geoffrey didn't. If he is going to continue to ignore me, then there is nothing I can do."

She sighed, cocked her head, and looked at me.

"Daughter, you have much to learn about dealing with men. Tonight, however, is not the night for instruction. You have accepted an invitation, so you need to put your mind straight about the evening. Cotton has grown into a fine man."

"But I don't feel the same about him." Even I could hear the whining in my voice. Maybe Mother was right. Months had gone by without a kind word. *Wasn't it time to forget about Geoffrey?*

"How you feel about someone doesn't mean he wouldn't make a good husband."

A long and heavy sigh escaped before I could hold it back. Mother didn't know about the kisses Geoffrey and I had exchanged. And I wasn't sure whether I could tell her. After all, she was the one who had insisted I read *Pamela* and *Clarissa*.[5] Of course, all my friends had read the books as well, and their themes were the topic of many conversations during our all-female social occasions. Pamela, the heroine in the first novel, had been pursued by her employer, who wanted only to bed her. In the end, she was rewarded for her chaste behavior when he came to her with a suitable marriage proposal. Clarissa's ruinous fate was sealed when she ran away with her beau without the benefit of wedding vows. If I were to believe the author of those books, those kisses with Geoffrey would probably ensure that I remain a *feme sole*, unmarried, for life, or I would die feeble-minded. Neither was a future I desired.

✦

We strolled along Fish Street enjoying the early evening and one another's company. As long as thoughts of Geoffrey were out of my mind, being with Cotton was easy. He had spent as much time in our home as in his own when we were young, and consequently, we all viewed him as one of us. We talked, we joked. He was a friend, a fellow Weston. I didn't want to think of him as more than a friend, yet I couldn't ignore his attentiveness of the last several months.

Bostonians were still celebrating the repeal of the Stamp Act one week after the big celebration in the Common. Every few feet, it seemed we encountered revelers and needed to sidestep their antics. Carriage traffic was sporadic. Streets were clogged with persons drinking and conversing so much so that it was easier, and quicker, to walk than ride to one's destination.

Entering Faneuil Hall was like walking into a land of dreams. Oil lamps hung from the supporting beams and the flames flickered

---

[5] Richardson, Samuel. *Pamela; or, Virtue Rewarded.* 1740. *Clarissa; or The History of a Young Lady.* 1748.

in the polished glass. Some of the market stalls had been removed, giving space for a large dance floor; others had been converted into booths offering a variety of small bites: cured meat, cheeses, and sweets. Across the dance floor, stalls served wine and punch. One fellow was busy whipping cream for syllabubs and passing them out to guests one after another. Laughter punctuated the music at irregular intervals and the background hum of conversation was constant. At the far corner of the large room was a small orchestra that managed to fill the cavernous space with notes to a beloved tune.

Cotton turned into me and without saying a word, whisked me into the middle of the room where we joined others in a lively jig. Ladies in their colorful frocks swirled and twirled around their partner as they kept beat to the music. The air in the hall grew hot and stifling, but the band didn't stop between melodies, nor did we. As we were about to collapse from exhaustion, the ensemble ceased playing so all of us could rest and find refreshment. Long lines of thirsty dancers waited to purchase drinks, so Cotton guided me toward the door.

"Fresh air will do us good," he said.

He escorted me to a more secluded spot while he returned to find us a cool drink. I enjoyed a slight breeze blowing inland. The drink and the cooler air revived our merry spirits. A gibbous moon shone on whispery silver clouds against the dark sky and, in an instant, I felt a slight quiver in my stomach and my breath caught in my throat.

"Molly."

He had whispered my name so gently I thought I had imagined hearing it.

My stomach clenched. I feared looking at my escort. Geoffrey had spoken to me in this tone moments before he kissed me.

Cotton drew nearer and placed both his hands on my elbows, willing me to look up, to look into his eyes.

I dared not. Cotton was a friend. Only a friend. I couldn't allow him to kiss me. If he kissed me here, in the presence of all these others, I could be branded a hussy, a trollop! Even worse, it would signal to everyone a relationship that I didn't want. A relationship that could turn into a marriage I did not, could not, would not, allow. Not while my feelings for Geoffrey were still so strong.

"It's a lovely night, isn't it?" I said, stepping back from his warm body. "And the music is delightful as well. Don't you think?"
A sigh escaped Cotton's lips and his shoulders sank a bit. Disappointment tinged his voice though he tried to sound lighthearted.

"Nobody in the city has danced as much as we tonight."

Nothing more was said, but when we heard the musicians begin their next song, we returned to our places on the dance floor. Visions of Pamela and Clarissa danced alongside us.

June 1766

Eli Weston

An impromptu meeting of the Sons of Liberty convened at the Green Dragon the evening that the Declaratory Act was published. My younger brother Paul and I met up with Sam Adams and Benjamin Edes, publisher of the *Boston Gazette,* on the way to the tavern. Adams was his usual outspoken self, and even though we were still on the street, he voiced his opinions loudly.

"This act has no basis in the English Constitution! The very idea that any resolution or vote we take is considered null and void is rubbish! The constitution gives every British citizen the right to be represented in Parliament, but it appears that once again, Parliament has acted without representing those who do not reside on that side of the Atlantic! How could you publish this farcical attempt at governance?"

"Sam, Sam," said Edes, "don't kill the messenger! The Stamp Act has come and gone; this Declaratory Act doesn't even mention taxes."

"That is precisely the issue, Ben. That which is not spelled out in law is left to interpretation, and I do not have faith that Parliament is of a mind to do what is best for the colonies. Heed my words, this tax issue has not been laid to rest."

By the time we reached the Green Dragon, the Sons of Liberty meeting was well underway. We heard the second-floor rumblings as soon as we entered the tavern. An occasional shout punched through to the first floor, giving rise to a louder undertone. As we climbed the stairs, tobacco smoke mixed with the soot from the oil lamps and fireplace ash to create a purplish haze that hung over our heads. We pushed our way through the dimly lit room to where a crowd surrounded Dr. Warren who was deep in discussion with Paul Revere and William Molineux.

"It's a travesty! Parliament has no right to vacate our laws. I can't believe that Parliament would repeal one heinous act of taxation and introduce in its stead another that has the potential to nullify anything and everything we try to do to govern ourselves. That, my friend, is the issue at hand we must discuss."

Adams, never one to hold back on his words, jumped into the discussion and pounded the table. "This is worse than being taxed without proper representation! Parliament has completely disregarded the rights of its citizenry. We colonies demand the right of self-governance. We demand the right to preserve our property.

"Does a lord know that his vote for taxation steals the food from our babies' mouths? No! Does a lord know that a tax on molasses does harm to every family? Does a lord know why we need molasses? Does he know that we use it for cooking and preserving food? No! He thinks we only use the West Indies concoction for making rum!"

Cries of Huzzah! Huzzah! responded to Sam's rant, which encouraged him further. Edes caught my eye and winked. Sam was only beginning his boisterous tirade, so we removed ourselves to a far corner where we could continue our earlier conversation.

"You'll read soon enough, Eli, that Bernard isn't giving up so easily."

"Governor Bernard and Lt. Governor Hutchinson will never come close to agreeing with us. They have spent too many years lining their purses with money harvested from the seeds others have sown."

"As well as that income gleaned from the government offices they and their family members hold."

"And have held," I added.

Ben Edes nodded.

"Bernard's clerk dropped off an advice today to print in Monday's edition. The likes of which will set Boston afire once more."

This tidbit piqued my curiosity. Adams was always in a snit about something, and calming him down was a regular occurrence. Now, Edes was telling me that Sam may be right . . . again.

"Bernard holds two letters from Secretary Conway as well as copies of the two Acts," Edes continued. "The first, of course, is the repeal of the Stamp Act —"

"Which we've been celebrating!"

"And the second is the Declaratory Act, which we've published. But it is this letter from Bernard that will set Adams off to find Molineux. Prepare for more unrest."

Ben fumbled in his breast pocket searching for something. Once found, he unfolded a piece of paper and began to read aloud the speech that Governor Bernard would be making to the Massachusetts Bay Colony Assembly the following day. It was full of all the pomp Bernard typically included in his addresses, but this particular speech was also full of condescension and contempt for his constituency.

Bernard's speech concluded with words that would, I agreed, rile the citizenry: "I am also ordered to recommend to you, that full and ample compensation be made to the late Sufferers by the Madness of the People."[6]

---

[6] *Boston-Gazette, and Country Journal,* June 9, 1766.

Molly Weston

Geoffrey continued to rant about The Declaratory Act whenever he came around the kitchen. No longer did he show me any affection, and I was slowly becoming accustomed to the loss of attention; his only concern these days was how this new act of Parliament would be the end of the Massachusetts Bay Colony's freedom. His judgment was sound in other matters so I kept quiet and listened. His father kept writing, and through him, we learned that although America had supporters in Parliament, there was growing resentment towards the colonies and their insistence in determining which taxes should be levied as well as how many, but there also was talk of other laws that could be enacted during the coming session of Parliament.

In late June, travelers from the western border brought news of unrest amongst the farmers. As I laid out trenchers of stew one afternoon, a man wearing the road on his clothes asked for a few extra biscuits.

"How many shall I bring? Is your hunger that great?"

His eyes looked at me and then down at the table.

Feeling a bit puzzled, I leaned over as a muddy paw stretched out to scratch at the bench leg.

"Oh, goodness! You poor thing!" I kneeled and reached under the table to pull out a small coffee-colored puppy. Ribs striped his young hide, and as I examined him, two coal-black eyes softened my heart.

"We can do better than biscuits, little fellow." Without hesitation, and without asking his owner, I whisked the hungry creature off to the kitchen.

At seeing me cradling another dog, Boots grumbled a bit and arose from his bed near the hearth to trot after us.

A quarter-hour and a few morsels of meat later, I returned the sated puppy to its owner and sat down before handing over the drowsy animal. I pulled several biscuits from my apron pocket and laid them beside the traveler's trencher.

"For you. If you're as hungry as this little fellow, you'll need them."

"It's been a long time since anyone showed us a bit of kindness, miss. We lost our farm and have been looking for a place to settle."

"Where did you come from?"

"Near the border with New York. Been walking for days." The traveler paused to shove a biscuit into his mouth.

"How did you lose your farm? Maybe I shouldn't be asking, but you and your puppy have come an awfully long way to find a new home. And unfortunately, there's not much work here."

Before he could reply, Eli plopped down on the bench across from the traveler and leaned across the table as if to exchange a confidence.

"Where did you say you came from? Down at the docks there's rumors of farmers being run off their land."

"That's not rumor, it's truth. In the Hudson River Valley, we don't own the land, yet we're the ones been tilling and harvesting, building homes and barns, corncribs and pens. We paid for the lumber, cleared the stones, made a farm where there wasn't one. We paid rent and turned over our share of crops to the manor lords, but every year, it cost us more and more. Then one day, the manor lords decided we hadn't paid enough and turned us out."

"They can't do that!"

"Molly, shush. Let the man speak."

The traveler took a long drink from his mug and then paused, his face wearing the inner struggle of his emotions.

"At first, we thought the manor lords meant only to force us to pay a higher rent, so we stayed. We looked for ways to get the money, but it was too much to pay. William Prendergast talked us into protesting the rents. Soon enough, a whole brigade of lobster backs is rousting the farms. They didn't attack only us, they attacked every farmer, every family. They charged in, broke up the furniture, threw out everything we had. Some even chased the women and young'uns into the woods . . ."

I gasped at hearing of the insolence of the soldiers and how they disregarded women and children, treating them worse than farm animals.

"We lost everything. They killed the livestock, stole whatever we couldn't carry, and smashed what they didn't want."[7]

The farmer paused. Remembering the incident was distressing our guest, and to comfort him, I reached out to touch his elbow. For some reason, I needed to know what happened.

"We gathered our men and set out for the city. By the time we reached New York, we numbered about 1,700. Called ourselves the   Levelers."

"Why head to New York?" asked Eli.

"We figured that if we had the Sons of Liberty on our side, the governor-in-chief, Henry Moore, would have to listen to our claim to the land." He curled his lip at the memory.

"Sons of Liberty!" Spittle flew from his mouth. "The Accursed Sons of the City is more like it."

Eli and I exchanged curious glances.

---

[7] Nash, G. B. 2005. The unknown American Revolution: The unruly birth of democracy and the struggle to create America. New York: NY: Viking Penguin.

"They wouldn't let us into the city. They blocked the road with soldiers. Freedom for them only." He spat on the floor, cursing the New York group.

"Who sent those soldiers?" Eli demanded.

"The governor's council."

The traveler suddenly turned his face to the table, hunched over his trencher, and began shoveling spoonsful of stew into his mouth. I looked at Eli who nodded and indicated to the door with his chin. Lt. Geoffrey Canfield had entered The Three Lions.

Geoffrey Canfield

I was looking forward to slaking my thirst at with ale at The Three Lions, but no sooner had I sat down then Molly came flying across the room.

"Come with me!" She grabbed my arm and, in a surprising show of strength, nearly toppled me from the bench before I could rise.

"What do you know about this?" She gestured wildly at a beggarly looking fellow across the room.

"I don't know who that is! What are you talking about?"

She began to relate the sordid tale and I sat back down to give it my full attention.

During one of our more recent meetings, General Bridgewater had informed us that General Thomas Gage, newly named Commander-in-Chief of the British Army in the colonies, had marched 250 British soldiers into the Hudson River Valley, ostensibly to quell some rioting tenant farmers who had begun to rise up against their manor lords. Bridgewater had made it sound as if the farmers were hardheaded misers who didn't want to pay their rents. But the severity of the rebuke was unconscionable. How professional soldiers could ransack belongings and treat women and children so poorly was a black mark on all of us who wore the King's red and white uniform.

Gage had been in New York for some time, and from all accounts, the New York colony admired him for his good nature and humor. I had to question, however, the wisdom of an extreme show of force. An action of this nature could derail all the good will he had created. The Stamp Act and the civil unrest it had incited were still fresh wounds for many colonists. Such severe retribution against individuals who were struggling to make a living wasn't a sound military tactic. It was possible that there were other issues of which we hadn't been informed, yet when I looked at that poor fellow and heard the passion in Molly's voice and saw the fire in her eyes, I knew that the King's military had erred in its judgment against the colonists once again.

Listening to Molly gave me pause. Her concern for someone she met a few minutes ago flooded my consciousness and, in a moment, it opened my eyes to her essence. This tawny-haired beauty shouldered the concerns of others as if they were her own. At the same time, she would move one step beyond the emotion she faced; she returned kindness with affection and tolerance with patience. The fire in Molly's eyes had been doused; now I could see only the sorrow she bore on behalf of the farmers.

Perhaps I, too, had made an error in judgment regarding this young woman standing in front of me. Could it be that the kiss I saw her bestow on Cotton back at the mill was simply a gesture of thanks? I raised my hand to caress her cheek, to let her know that I cared, that I forgave her. But I stopped. Now was not the time. Later, perhaps, we could find another moment. It would need to be soon if I were to win back her heart.

July 1766

Molly Weston

After the May celebration and the ball, life returned to normal. I helped mother in the kitchen preparing for the day's meals, and then hurried off to assist in Anna's shop. The repeal of the Stamp Act had raised the spirits of all the women in town, and as such, there were many more women purchasing goods. Our latest shipment of linen gloves, perfect for warmer weather, was selling out quickly. Women who had been conserving their money now found more ways to spend it. Even the most frivolous of fripperies, such as the peacock feathered hats, were finding new homes with our wealthier clientele.

Mercy Otis Warren had made several stops at Anna's since we had met at the May celebration, and we often found ourselves discussing the latest fashions rather than politics.

"These panniers are getting so big they are ridiculous!" she began one day.

The elongated hoop forms that tied around one's waist gave the chemise and petticoat a wide silhouette from the waist down. Some of the most fashionable forms were so wide that a wearer needed to turn sideways in order to pass through a doorway.

"What nonsense! Whoever thought this would be a good idea should be made to wear one! How shall I dance? My arms aren't nearly long enough to reach my partner."

Anna and I giggled at her outburst. Mercy was known to speak her mind. She shared the gift of eloquence with her lawyer brother, James Otis, who recently had been elected to the Assembly.

"The fabrics of the gowns they are wearing in England are too beautiful for words. Imported silks are embroidered around the hem and on the sleeves, some go as far as embroidering around the neck, and then they match the chemise in fabric and embroidery! I remember seeing one gown that was simply stunning — it was a pale cream with white embroidery. Can you imagine wearing something so elegant in Boston with our streets of dirt and mud?"

"Perhaps we could find a more suitable brown silk with black embroidery floss," I countered, "to better hide the muck stains?"

Mercy's laughter held no bounds. In the store, she lost all refinement of her breeding and became another of us middling sort.

"Hmm. Brown silk would definitely resolve the problem, but how dull it would be to see all the women in such unimaginative dress. Would our men be able to find us in a crowd? Speaking of crowds, what shall you wear for the upcoming holiday?"

Governor Bernard had declared July 24 to be a colony wide day to celebrate the repeal of the Stamp Act. Once again, everyone was making plans for another day of merrymaking at the Common. There was talk of the fishermen bringing in lobsters and cod, and the women were already baking specialty breads and cakes to share. Father had set aside a hogshead of ale, a contribution from The Three Lions.

Cotton continued to come around more and more frequently. Evidently, my reluctance to kiss him hadn't deterred him in his courtship ritual. Every Saturday, he returned from logging, sponged the dirt off his face and arms, and made his way to the tavern. Once there, he sat and drank, and talked, and ate, and talked some more till late at night. His ventures at witty conversation with his companions weren't always successful, and at times, it was painfully obvious that his forays into the ongoing discussions were meant to impress me.

Geoffrey Canfield

It was Saturday night, yet another weekend evening where Cotton was expounding on topics of which he knew little, if anything.

Eli and I sat at our customary table in the far corner and observed his best friend.

"How do these absurdities occur to him?" I asked Eli. "Can he not hear what spouts from his mouth?"

My friend sighed and swigged his ale before answering.

"Cotton has never been one for learning. He got by at school because of my help, but he never showed much interest. His attention always lay in physical activity, not the mental. Hence, his ability to excel at logging."

"But look at him! How can your sister be interested in such a ne'er-do-well?"

"Geoffrey! Your green-eyed monster is raising his ugly head. Best to be off to bed if you can't tolerate his presence."

"Oh, I can tolerate him, it's the foolishness that spews forth that I cannot abide."

I tore my eyes off my competitor and searched for my beloved. For months, I had avoided any interaction with her, and yet, my heart remained bound to her. We lived in the same house. She served me meals in the kitchen. And although I hadn't behaved as a lover should have after the mill had exploded, not being able to spend time alone with her had pierced my soul like a rapier through my heart. It's true she had tried to draw close and I had been the one to pull back. But that kiss! I simply could not erase from my mind the image of seeing her kiss Cotton.

Bah! If she were to choose another, let her. I could, I would forever remain a bachelor.

Still, those eyes that sparkle when she smiles! No, I will not give up. I will fight to regain her love.

First, however, I must best my rival.

Molly Weston

Heavens! Cotton was back at the tavern, carousing with his friends. Eli, I had noticed, no longer sat with Cotton. Instead, he opted for a quieter table where he was often joined by Geoffrey.

"Molly! Another ale!"

I located the loud drunkard and wove my way through the partying crowd to deposit a fresh tankard of ale.

"Molly! Here too!"

That voice I recognized. Cotton. It was as if he knew exactly when I would have a free moment, and he made use of those moments to occupy my time.

"Sit with us a bit, Molly," he cajoled when I laid out the ales. "Everyone deserves a moment of rest."

"Yes, everyone does. But not this everyone and not right now. Enjoy your ale, gentlemen."

"Molly!" His tone was sharper than before. So much so, and so unlike him, that I spun around and glared.

He was on his feet and already moving towards me. I couldn't but help to take a step back.

"No, no. The drink has gone to my head. Do not fear me."

"Cotton, perhaps it is best for you to turn in for the night."

"Perhaps. But not before I can speak with you in private. I need, no, I mean I want, no that's not it either."

"Speak your mind, Cotton. I have other customers to attend, and we are old enough friends to be frank with one another."

"No, perhaps I shall come 'round in the morning once my head as cleared. Good night, dear Molly."

He stepped in close, and before I could react, he cupped my face in his hands and brushed his lips across my forehead. And then, in an instant, he was gone.

The speed with which he acted was surprising, given the amount of drink he had consumed. Yet even more surprising was the display of public affection he had shown. I wasn't sure whether I was to be angry or offended at such boldness. Confused, definitely.

Paul, who had been expecting Cotton to collect him to head back into the logging camp, opened the door the next morning. A most contrite Cotton appeared at the kitchen entryway, looking as if he had been scolded by the schoolmaster. Hat in hand, had he owned one.

There was no way to remain angry when confronted by such a spectacle. I laughed and pulled him into a chair at the table.

"Eat. Then speak."

I busied myself in the kitchen while the tall blond ate. Mostly he picked at the food, occasionally sipping at the hot mug of coffee I had placed on the table. Truly he was a sorry sort that morning.

Finally, the most pressing of the morning chores done, I sat opposite him. He raised his head, his eyes regarding me with a most sincere and chastised gaze. There was a thoughtfulness in those blue eyes that I hadn't noticed before, an earnestness heretofore unknown to me.

"I apologize for my outburst last evening. The boys and I drank a bit much and, I daresay, it went to my head."

I smiled, but said nothing. After a moment's silence, he began again.

"You have always had a place in my heart, Molly. Even as children, you were the girl who charmed me. It seemed that you felt the same for me."

"Oh, Cotton!" My breath left my chest with such a force that I felt I should faint. Such a declaration of affection was unexpected. That he had perceived my fondness for him was inconceivable. Boys, men, males were not supposed to understand such feelings!

"Surely you know that I have developed feelings for you, too. Is it possible that your heart has room for me? At least a pigeonhole where I could lay claim?"

"Cotton," I smiled. "When declaring yourself to a woman, it is preferable to not compare her heart to a nest for birds."

He reddened a bit, but his earnestness was intensifying. He leaned across the table and clasped my hands. The cracked, calloused hands were rough and scratched my palms, but I didn't dare to pull them away. Such an action would have caused him such hurt.

"Attend the holiday celebrations with me."

Pictures of the ball two months ago filled my head. So much dancing, so much fun. Until he tried to kiss me. The guilt I felt at that moment had eased somewhat, but it came roaring back in full force last night. My feelings for Geoffrey were still strong, and until I could reconcile those feelings with those I had once felt for Cotton, I wasn't sure whether I should accompany my old friend.

So, I sat across the table and contemplated my friend and his request.

"Yes."

I just couldn't say no. There was only one way to determine how I felt about Cotton, and that would be to spend more time with him. Thursday would be a day to remember.

✦

For the second time in as many months, Cotton collected me and we strolled toward the Common where spicy aromas mingled with sweet on the evening's breeze. Fishermen were boiling barrels of lobster and cod and bakers had set up tables of savory breads and delectable cookies, muffins, and cakes. A variety of stands offered raisins, figs, and other fruits one could easily eat while perusing the stalls and taking part in games of chance. All of Boston had turned out for Bernard's special holiday. Every chance we had to enjoy our victory over Parliament was sweet.

The dread I had anticipated at being with Cotton disappeared once I had decided to give him another chance. That decision lifted the burden of guilt, and I could free myself to be entertained and appreciated by a handsome admirer. We promenaded around the Common, encountering many friends who were also celebrating.

We chanced upon Hester Gardner, who pranced alongside her beau. My friend was resplendent in a rose-colored calico dress and white neck kerchief with contrasting lace. As always, her dress complimented her blue eyes and corn-silk hair.

"Oh, Molly. Don't you look grand! Why, hello, Cotton!" Hester winked at me.

"I'm no longer a Gardner, you know," she continued. "Thank heavens the Stamp Act was repealed or Cyrus and I would never have been married! I simply adore being Mrs. Winslow!"

"Mmm, yes, of course," I mumbled. Hester, for all her supposedly endearing qualities, always had a way of insinuating herself into a situation with her words, and now was the perfect instance of her meddlesome behavior. Her approach was always one of friendship, but a darker intent lurked that would, eventually and at an unexpected moment, emerge to sting her prey.

"Why don't we go around together? It will be so much fun for us to catch up and the men can entertain us with their ability at games!"

The last thing I wanted was to spend time with this garrulous girl, but Hester never allowed a victim to withdraw once she had made a decision. Her hand wrapped around my elbow, and with the strength of an eagle's talons, she led me away to look at a display of silk kerchiefs, leaving her new spouse looking as bewildered as was Cotton.

As I suspected, after we had taken a few steps, she leaned in.

47

"When I saw you with Cotton, I knew I had to find out what happened to that lovely lieutenant you had been seeing last year."

I knew I was blushing for the heat on my neck and throat intensified internally.

"Hester, I'm not quite sure what you are referring to." I picked up a kerchief and closely examined the stitching. Nonchalance was my best defense now.

"Oh, you poor thing! With all your work, you really have been away from all sorts of gossip."

My emotions spun round and round and up and down as if in a butter churn. What could she be talking about? Had people seen Geoffrey and me kissing? Had they seen Cotton try to kiss me? My fears about being labeled a hussy for improper behavior might be coming true. I felt my stomach lurch.

"Are you feeling ill?" A strong hand grasped my elbow as my knees began to buckle.

"No, I'll be fine. It must be this heat."

I raised my head and found myself looking into Geoffrey's eyes. The deep blue irises twinkled and I audibly gasped. My surprise must have been overheard by everyone.

Geoffrey was smiling at me. He didn't release my arm, and suddenly I became aware of the passage of time. Cotton quickly stepped up to intercede, while Hester watched the small drama and smiled from behind a fan. Cyrus simply looked distracted.

"Thank you, but I'll see her home." Cotton's voice carried a serious undertone.

"As is proper." Geoffrey nodded slightly at the four of us and backed away, his eyes boring through my pretense and into my soul.

August 1766

Eli Weston

I hadn't seen my British friend for several days when he strode into the tavern and, upon seeing me, grinned as I had never seen before. He slid onto the bench in front of me, grabbed my tankard, and drained it. He slammed the vessel onto the table and laughed.

"It's done!"

"You'll have to explain yourself, Canfield. How much 'done' is done?"

He chuckled. "It was perfect. I couldn't have hoped for a better beginning than what happened. And I owe it all to Hester Winslow."

"Who? What did she do?"

"Used to be Hester Gardner, one of Molly's friends. She was promenading with her husband when they chanced upon Molly and Cotton."

I winced at hearing Hester's name. "And what were you doing that you saw all this happen?"

"Patrolling, of course. But it was the perfect means of ensuring Molly's safety."

"You mean to say you spied on my sister."

"Pshaw! Only to ensure that nothing untoward happened. As it was, my proximity enabled me to step in and catch her as she was about to faint."

"Faint? Molly isn't the fainting sort."

"Perhaps not, but I've yet to see anyone paler than she who could still stand upright."

I tried to imagine Molly fainting. Perhaps he was right. Her constitution had seemed frailer after the mill incident.

"This time I was the hero," Geoffrey whispered softly to himself.

Geoffrey Canfield

The colonists held so many celebrations upon learning that the Stamp Act had been repealed that part of me was beginning to think they were daft. Two months after the May celebrations, Governor Bernard called for the entire Massachusetts Bay Colony to recognize the holiday. I questioned Bernard's reason to call for a celebration of an event so far removed from the actual date.

For as much time as I spent pondering Bernard's reasoning, my black boots were getting a healthy shine. I lined them up underneath the chair, then folded the polishing cloth into quarters and laid it next to them. A knock on the door roused me from my thoughts, and I padded to the door in stockinged feet.

Eli quickly stepped in and in a hushed voice urged me to dress and meet him at the Green Dragon. The urgency in his voice and concern in his eyes convinced me that I needed to take care. Hurriedly I donned an old cloak and wide-brimmed hat that Henry had found for me. In this disguise, I would be able to walk the streets without being recognized for what I was, a British soldier, and a traitor to the Crown.

By the time we had arrived at the Dragon, a small crowd had already gathered. Various merchants, members of the Sons of Liberty, whispered vehemently. Some were jabbing fingers in the air to compensate for the inability to raise their voices. The men shushed themselves once John Hancock entered the room.

Hancock was one of the wealthiest men in Boston. He had purchased the second largest wharf in the port and operated a sizeable ship-building facility. Although it wasn't spoken aloud, everyone knew that his uncle Thomas had built the family fortunes by smuggling and that John had carried on the tradition. To British eyes, however, Hancock was the paragon of businessmen, and the reason for all of us meeting late at night.

"Earlier today, I received a letter from fellow merchants in Britain, who have joined together to advise us Americans regarding the Stamp Act," he began.

I looked at Eli, who nodded and motioned with his head for me to continue to listen.

"These merchants are audacious enough to tell us that we should be satisfied with the Act's repeal. Yet in the same letter, they let us know that Parliament has declined to issue paper money, no, let me be more precise. Parliament has *postponed* issuing paper currency."

Sam Adams jumped to his feet.

"We know what that means! They have no intention of issuing currency. They'll have us eat our young before they print!"

"Sam, calm down. Let John finish."

"Thank you, Eli. It's not only the issuance of currency, neither will they respond to our request to import wine, fruit, and oil directly from other countries. We must continue to pay heavy tariffs on these items."

The crowd was growing louder with each sentence, and I feared that our clandestine meeting would be reported. I circulated throughout the room to hush the listeners so that Hancock could finish.

"The merchants have deemed it the duty of *Americans* to supply the Crown with raw materials so that *Great Britain's* manufactory may continue. Our fellow merchants," Hancock's words now carried the mark of sarcasm, "our fellow merchants are urging us to consider the benefit of Britain's manufactory, not America's. Our raw material is for Britain's use, no one else's, not even our own."

At that statement, Adams once again leapt to his feet, but this time he was joined by Molineux and others. There was no containing anyone at this point, so I carefully worked my way close to the back stairs should I need to escape quickly.

"In a word, the system of Great Britain is to promote a mutual interest by supplying the colonies with her manufactures, by encouraging them to raise, and receiving from them all raw materials, and by granting the largest extension to every branch of their trade not interfering with her own,"[8] he concluded.

William Molineux, himself a merchant, distilled the meaning quickly enough. "They want to line their purses at our expense!"

Upon hearing those words, I departed apace. The crowd's noise was deafening, and I didn't dare to be found in their company lest they decide on more punitive action towards a member of the Royal Army.

---

[8] *Boston-Gazette, and Country Journal*, September 9, 1766.

Molly Weston

Running into Hester and Cyrus was unfortunate, but then having Geoffrey step in to support me stoked her fire, to say the least. It was my escort, Cotton, who should have come to my aid, but he was several paces behind with Cyrus. My friend Hester. Oh, how I wish I had never come across her at the Common! I couldn't help but wonder whether she had engineered the encounter between Geoffrey, Cotton, and me. That woman never acted impetuously. Every activity, every word was planned. She thrived on gossip and sought out the most loquacious of the harpies to spread her poison. I had seen her shred reputations with her razor-sharp tongue, and now I feared that I had become the next target. I wasn't sure how anything I had done would merit such abusive attention, but Hester was always doing something devious. Again, the thought occurred to me: Could she have shaped our meeting so that Geoffrey would be available?

So many details were involved: ensuring that Cotton and Cyrus were occupied, steering the conversation to topics I was sensitive to, knowing that Geoffrey would be at the Common, including knowing that Cotton and I would be attending together! I screamed silently in frustration. Thinking in this manner would drive me to lunacy, and I vowed to put such thoughts away. *That day's events unfolded as they were supposed to, without anyone's ulterior motives, and the outcome was a result of sheer coincidence, nothing more.*

Nothing, I thought, until several evenings later when I walked into the tavern's great room late one evening and right into a quarrel between Geoffrey and Cotton. The men were toe-to-toe, spittle flying from their mouths as they roared at one another.

"You managed all of it!"

"You haven't any idea of what I may or may not have done!"

"There it is! You admit it!" Cotton jabbed his finger at Geoffrey.

"I'll admit to nothing! You're fabricating stories to feel better about not being there when she needed you."

At this last remark, Cotton pulled back his right hand, balled it into a fist, and landed a heavy blow to Geoffrey's temple. Geoffrey stumbled backward, but quickly recovered to deliver a jaw-cracking punch of his own. Cotton's head snapped back and blood spurted from his nose.

Eli and Paul raced across the room to separate the foes, and I retreated to the hearth, wishing I could disappear into its flames.

Whatever are they thinking fighting like that, and in the tavern with everyone watching? No sooner had that thought crossed my mind than I espied Cyrus Winslow sitting in the far corner, a smug smile spreading across his face. Of all the people to witness this! By tomorrow, the entire town would know of the row in The Three Taverns. So artful were her wiles that without even being present, Hester had triumphed. My mortification was complete.

September 1766

Molly Weston

It wasn't but a week after learning about Prendergast and the Levelers from the itinerant farmer that we read about the former's trial in the *Gazette*. Prendergast's sentence, however, gave me pause:

> That the Prisoner be led back again to the Place from whence he came, and from thence shall be drawn on a Hurdle to the Place of Execution, and there shall be hanged by the Neck, and then shall be cut down alive, and his Entrails and Privy Members shall be cut from his Body, and shall be burned in his Sight, and his Head shall be cut off, and his Body shall be divided into four Parts, and shall be disposed at the King's Pleasure . . .[9]

"Inconceivable. That in this day such a barbaric execution be practiced on someone simply for defending one's property and right to earn a living."

"What's that?"

"This Prendergast affair, Eli. The jury found him guilty of high treason and has seen fit to not only hang him, but to have him drawn and quartered. A 'jury of some of the most respectable Freeholders of the county' indeed! Such savages! And they would have us regard them in high esteem and obey laws that they enacted specifically to protect themselves and their property."

---

[9] *Boston-Gazette, and Country Journal*, September 8, 1766.

"Stop your pacing! You're making me dizzy."

No sooner had I sat than my brother stood up and began to trace my own steps around the kitchen.

"Found guilty of high treason and the appropriate punishment was given, according to the courts."

My brother was thinking aloud, a habit developed while attending Latin School to learn his lessons. I knew that a response wasn't needed nor desired. He would indicate when my opinion was appropriate.

"The prosecutor calls for mercy, and the jury says otherwise. A jury not of peers but of landholders, men against whom the defendant was protesting."

The eldest of my brothers fell silent though he continued to grind into powder the sand dusted across the floor.

"Molly, I need to talk to Sam."

Indeed. Sam Adams definitely would have an opinion on the New York affair.

Eli Weston

Prendergast and his Levelers had risen up against the unjust conduct of the manor lords of Dutchess County in New York. What had begun as tenant farmers leasing land from the Wappinger Indians had turned into one family, the Philips's, receiving a court injunction against the Indians. The family promptly began to eject the farmers, with the court's blessing, from the land they had cultivated for generations. The charge of high treason against Prendergast was based on his inability and unwillingness to allow such an injustice to remain the law of the land.

Molly was right. It was inconceivable that a leader of the common man should suffer such a reprehensible execution. Thanks to her keen eye, we had been warned of the punishment awaiting us should we continue to resist Parliament's latest governing decrees. Acts of treason met with the severest of punishments. Death.

Geoffrey Canfield

The morning of September 24th, General Bridgewater called me to his office located in a brick house rented from one of Boston's wealthier merchants. It was customary of officers to appropriate homes in which to live while serving abroad as they often brought their wives and children to their field of service. I wasn't privy to know where the home's owner now abided. This particular house had a commodious front room in which the general conducted most of his business. The wall behind him featured an oversized portrait of someone I didn't know, a rotund gentleman whose head all but exploded out of a tight collar. I could barely make out the signature to be that of Boston's contribution to art, John Singleton Copley. To the general's left and between two windows overlooking Beacon Street and the Common, a tall free-standing clock ticked away the minutes and, to his right, a fireplace was laden with wood and kindling, ready for a match to warm away the evening chill.

I still hadn't fully come to terms with his attitude towards me after we had demolished his munitions cache at that abandoned mill. It had been nearly a year now, and the fury I had expected to rain down on me still hadn't fallen. I wasn't sure whether the man was simply biding his time to exact his revenge or he was simply too oblivious to the activities of his officers to know that I had been a part of that action.

"Lt. Canfield, we have received word from a Loyalist that another smuggler is operating in the city."

The absurdity of hearing those words out of the mouth of one who had commanded his own smuggling ring! I fixed my eyes on the painted gentleman's curled wig and bit my cheek to maintain a stoic presence.

The corpulent general shuffled some papers on the desk, found what he was searching for, and thrust it into my hands.

I wasn't surprised to hear that more smuggling was occurring. Several times a week we received information about someone who was smuggling wine, molasses, or some other item. Never was the accuser named in the writ, and that anonymity bothered me. Loyalists were exploiting the system to punish fellow citizens who had objected to the Stamp Act. It was my own opinion that the Loyalists had as many hands in smuggling as the Patriots, and by punishing those who held different beliefs, they could continue to profit.

The name on the writ concerned me. Daniel Malcolm.[10] I knew Malcolm to be a model of the Americans who built up their fortunes from nothing but their own desire and hard work. He started as a sailor, worked up to ship's captain, and now was a merchant. The Writ of Assistance in my hands claimed that Malcolm was storing smuggled wine and liquor in his house. Our orders were to search the premises, confiscate the goods, and arrest the smuggler. I had no choice other than to lead the raid. But first, I needed to get word to Eli.

---

[10] Carp. B. L. 2007. Rebels rising: Cities and the American Revolution. New York, NY: Oxford University Press.

Eli Weston

"Eli! Eli!"

I turned at hearing young Henry calling me. Ever since our brother Paul had left his employ at The Three Lions, Henry had stepped up to fill his shoes. Hence, it was rare to find my youngest brother outside of the tavern. Whatever brought him out must be important.

He reached me and huffed a few breaths before he could relay the message.

"Canfield. Orders. Malcolm."

I looked at him and tried to decipher the puzzling words. In a flash, I knew what he was trying to say.

"Daniel Malcolm?"

Henry nodded, still trying to catch his breath.

"Go there now, and quickly. Maybe there is time to stop this before it goes any further."

Malcolm lived in the North End, and Long Wharf was halfway to the South End. Henry would have to hurry if he were to warn Malcolm. I took off in another direction, to find John Matchet, a friend of Malcolm's from when they were both seafaring captains, and Benjamin Goodwin, whose distillery was nearby. We would need as many men as possible to show our opposition.

Thanks to Henry's swift legs, Malcolm was able to draw a small crowd to defend his home. Paul Revere, another North Ender, and William McKay had joined him. McKay had more reason than others to aid Malcolm as he, too, was a Patriot merchant and could easily suffer the same unwarranted search. Filling out the band of protection were boys from the grammar school. The young lads looked anxious and perhaps a bit frightened at not knowing what to expect, but through their uncertainty shone a bravado at being able to stand up to tyrannical searches. I prayed that none of them would be hurt in the violence sure to follow.

Malcolm, Revere, McKay, and I stepped to the front of the pack, forming a first line of defense. Matchet and Goodwin and several of the larger boys aligned as our seconds. The remainder, including the grammar school lads, spread out along the edges to get a better view of the soon-to-be confrontation.

Our intent was to talk. We hoped that Canfield would be able to act as an intelligent individual and not as an armed officer of His Majesty's Royal Army. Within moments, we heard the approaching march of Canfield's squad. A platoon of redcoats turned the corner, and we braced ourselves.

Canfield's eyes met mine and I detected a glimmer of hope. Maybe there wouldn't be any blood shed today.

Geoffrey Canfield

An unusually large chattering of jackdaws perched in the trees before their flight south. Blue and green glistened off their dark feathers as they tilted their heads from side to side. Their strident *chakking* pierced the air as they watched the scenario below.

I breathed a bit easier when I saw Eli standing next to Daniel Malcolm. Henry had kept his word and spread the news about the most recently issued Writ. I raised my right hand to signal my squad to halt, but I continued walking toward the group. It had been my intent for Eli to assemble a large crowd, and he had delivered.

"We have orders to search the premises of Daniel Malcolm."

I awaited their reply. Spoken or physical. It would be up to Eli and his group to initiate the use of force.

When it had looked as if the issuance of Writs of Assistance were to become commonplace, Eli and I worked out a plan of action. To reinforce my loyalty to the Crown in the eyes of my soldiers and my superiors, I needed to maintain a distance from the Americans charged with breaking the law, yet my allegiance to the Americans required me to use my position to assist the accused from these deleterious allegations.

I surveyed the group Eli and Henry had amassed. A shabby crowd, certainly, but every face expressed determination and defiance. Down to the small ones, who probably were no more than ten years in age. In their hands were instruments of destruction and pain, cudgels and hammers, and pockets bulged with what must have been rocks to sling at us. No, they couldn't match my troops in munitions, but they could damage us all the same.

As I wondered who would speak for the crowd, the silversmith Revere stepped forward.

"We object to this Writ. Malcolm demands to know who has named him. According to the Bible, even the Romans allowed the accused the right to face his accuser."

"Mr. Revere, we are here only to carry out the instructions in the Writ, that is, to search the premises of Mr. Malcolm. Any question regarding the origin of the Writ must be taken up with Lt. Governor Hutchinson."

"Ha!"

The mention of Hutchinson drew guffaws from the older men in the crowd. Many in the colony despised the Lt. Governor for his allegiance to the Crown's interests over those of his countrymen.

Boots shuffled in the dirt behind me. My men were getting restless. I scanned the crowd in front of me. Some of the boys' hands had disappeared into their pockets to finger the rocks stored within. Eli's mob outnumbered us two to one. Against so many, our weapons could injure, maim, and even kill, but we too would suffer casualties. More than the injuries, I feared the uproar if any of the boys were to be harmed.

A pebble danced at my feet. Instantaneously, I could hear the commotion of soldiers raising their muskets.

"Hold fire!"

From the corner of my eye, I glimpsed a young boy at the far edge of the group smirking. As I turned to look, he stared into my eyes and deliberately removed a larger stone from his right pocket and bounced it in his palm. Again, I sought out Eli. He would need to step in soon if we were to get out of this confrontation peacefully.

"There'll be no more of that." Eli, too, had found the miscreant and, without a second to spare, snatched the rock and threw it to the side.

"Our quarrel is with Parliament, not with you. Leave us be."

I nodded, turned the soldiers around, and marched from Malcolm's domicile.

October 1766

Molly Weston

Eli and Geoffrey were playing a game of cat and mouse with the city magistrates. The confrontation between the two groups in front of Daniel Malcolm's house was but one example. They had managed to escape serious injury, but I felt that Providence would not always shine so brightly on their efforts. The tale that Geoffrey and Eli told of the confrontation didn't quite match what Edes and Gills published in the *Gazette* and I laughed at reading the comparison:

> The customhouse officers were refus'd admittance by Capt. Malcolmb, and retired---that there really were no goods in the house liable to a Seizure---and that as for the good People, who were *curious spectators,* they behav'd as orderly, to use the words of some of the Deponents, as if they were at church.[11]

I felt sure that no one was fooled by Ben's writing. Stories of what really happened had been circulating for several weeks. This morning's article about the upcoming trial served as an official recounting for those residing across the Atlantic who would never directly learn the truth.

The Writs were stoking the embers of disquiet in our little band of freedom seekers, but my worries about the activities of my

---

[11] *Boston Gazette and Country Journal*, October 27, 1766.

brothers, Geoffrey, and the other Sons of Liberty were put to rest when Eli came back from a meeting at Faneuil Hall with good news.

"The vote passed. We will be given the opportunity to correct those mistakes in the Writ against Daniel."

We had feared that the depositions given by those persons in league with the governor would prejudice anyone who would sit on the jury for Daniel Malcolm's trial. According to John Hancock, who served as Daniel's lawyer, many of these depositions contained inaccuracies but also opinions and speculations without basis in fact. Thankfully, Daniel would have James Otis, the Reverend Samuel Sewall, Sam Adams, as well as Hancock and a few others who would speak to the governor and correct some of the opinions that could prejudice the King's ministers.

"Now will you and Geoffrey stop these silly confrontations? The two of you have been fortunate that General Bridgewater is none the wiser as to your doings. But even more, I worry that, one of these days, either Geoffrey will lose control of his men, or your influence over whatever mob you muster will be disregarded."

"No matter your fears, dear sister, our duty is to ensure that Writs are not enforced. Parliament, and consequently, the governor and lieutenant governor have given magistrates and customs officers a loose rein, and they are riding rough over citizens. We cannot allow them to continue."

Geoffrey Canfield

Molly's preoccupation with Prendergast and the Levelers was unprecedented. Fortunately, it has given me occasion to speak with her and smooth the path to a renewed relationship.

We learned on October 6 that Prendergast did receive a reprieve from Sir Henry Moore, who deemed it necessary to learn the King's prerogative in the matter. Nevertheless, the postponement of the prisoner's death wasn't a large enough step to please many of his followers.

> A Number of Men, without the least Tumult, Noise or previous Notice, suddenly assembled at the Goal where he is confined, and offered to release and convey him to a Place of Safety: But he told them, that having received a Reprieve, he chose to remain where he was, and wait the Result. Besides he told them, if he should escape without any other Inconveniences, it would certainly be attended with the loss of his Property in this Government, which would reduce his Family to Poverty and Want.[12]

Of concern, too, in New York is the issue of the Liberty Pole. For the second time, it has been cut down, and a third pole erected in its stead. Nary a soul has been charged with the transgression; loyalists are as much a possibility as British regulars. All this questionable activity sits on top of the population's agitation in response to the Quartering Act. The entire city had decided to not house and feed British soldiers. According to my father's letters, their

---

[12] *Boston-Gazette, and Country Journal*, October 6, 1766.

defiance in this matter was creating a protest of its own amongst the members of Parliament.

Although our neighbors to the south are experiencing much anxiety, Boston, for the moment, has been enjoying a period of calm. While the city was at peace, I decided it was the moment for me to move forward with Molly.

Recalling the first time I had sought her out, I chose once again to encounter her on the street. Perhaps a chance meeting would provoke fonder memories of the two of us and provide the opening for me to request her company. A public venue would ease her mind as we wouldn't be supplying grist for wagging tongues.

Hester Winslow

I haven't seen much of Molly since the Stamp Act celebrations, but then, I had been spending my time cultivating acquaintances who could be of assistance in bettering our social standing. Mercy Otis Warren had caught my attention during the festivities, and she was exactly the sort of woman I could fashion myself after. Arranging a chance meeting, however, proved more difficult than I had first thought. After days turned into weeks of strolling past her house with nary a sight of the woman, today I encountered her as she stepped out into the late afternoon sun.

The wind was brisk and the air cool, so the two of us were bundled in shawls and caps. Suddenly, a fierce gust whisked off her cap and sent it flying.

"Oh, no!" I gasped as the wind filled Mercy's white head covering and sent it even further aloft, soaring to the tips of the leafless elms.

"May I be of assistance?"

Mercy, ever of good humor, was chuckling at the situation. Not only had the wind sent her cap traveling, but it had also taken liberties with her styled hair. Medusa's serpentine locks held no comparison to the curls that once had been carefully coiffed and now were flying around her head.

"Oh, no. There's nothing to be done on a day like today," she laughed. "I'm sure I look frightful. Best I head inside before someone sees me."

She turned back once reaching the top of the stairs.

"Haven't we met before? I apologize for not remembering your name."

I gleefully pounced on this most favorable circumstance.

"Hester Winslow, Mrs. Warren. Both of us have attended several common social events lately. It's a delight to meet you, even if the circumstances aren't the best for introductions."

"Thank you for your kindness, Hester. Why don't you come in and join me for some refreshment? My errands can wait. Goodness, what am I saying? They have to wait, won't they? I can't be out in public looking like a scarecrow!"

Over tea and cookies, we conversed about Boston's upcoming social events, and I was able to convince Mrs. Warren that we shared many of the same interests. An hour later, when I took my leave of her, she urged me to call her Mercy. Being on a first-name basis with the sister of James Otis, a I left her home with my spirits high. Finally, I had met one of the city' most notable women.

Geoffrey Canfield

Eli and Ben Edes pushed by me and, before I could express my curiosity, Ben held up a sheaf of papers, an extensive letter to a gentleman in Hartford, and began to read aloud. The letter began with the expected niceties, but quickly deteriorated into a criticism of the Americans:

> But if . . . the repealing of the stamp act is received, considered and explained in America as condescension or submission, or extorted by the colonies, from sovereign, supreme authority---or if the occasion should be celebrated with extravagance, riot, and triumph, indicatory of such sentiments or opinion; then will the Americans be said here to have conspired in betraying their redeemers, & even of bringing them to *open shame,* and may not be only instrumental in overturning the present administration, but of introducing into North-America, a different police, founded in and supported with force and rigour.[13]

The hair on the back of my neck stood on end upon hearing those words. Suddenly the reasoning behind Bernard's declaration of a holiday two months after the fact had come to the forefront. With each celebration, Americans were seen to be shaming Parliament, and possibly the King. And each celebration gave the Crown more reason to assert its authority over the colonists.

---

[13] *Boston-Gazette, and Country Journal,* October 20, 1766.

"Do you think Governor Bernard is actively promoting dissension among the people so as to implement a more aggressive stance against them?"

"If we hadn't acted, our so-called friends abroad wouldn't have bothered themselves with our predicament."

"Most definitely," agreed Ben. "Boston needs to know what our 'upbraided patrons and advocates' in Great Britain are thinking. But it might be wiser to wait and see what Bernard and Hutchinson are planning. Gills and I've already decided to push off publishing this letter until we know more."

"What's done is done, Eli," I said. "The issue now is to closely watch Bernard. Along with Hutchinson and Peter and Andrew Oliver, he has the most to gain from maintaining close ties with the ministers of the Crown."

Eli Weston

Geoffrey is quite insightful for a soldier. For a British soldier on American soil. He's been here only a few years, yet has soaked up the sea of Boston politics much like a sponge in the ocean. He can intuit a response even before the question is asked, a defense before the provocation. He's the product of England. Raised an earl's son and schooled in strategy, and politics run thick in his blood.

As always, he was right about the Oliver's, Hutchinson, and Bernard being closer than a tarred man and his feathers. Andrew Oliver, the infamous stamp master whose effigy burned during the Stamp Act riots, and his brother Peter, shared a tangled relationship with Lt. Governor Hutchinson. Andrew had served in the Assembly alongside Hutchinson, and both of them had set about acquiring civil and political position. Office after office, sometimes serving in more than one office at a time and being paid for each. Together they climbed the ladder of power. After the Stamp Act riots had destroyed their houses, both families had lived at Castle William for several months. Peter's son had married Hutchinson's daughter, Sara, and his family mingled with the Hutchinson's socially. And as for Bernard, well, there probably wasn't a greedier fellow holding a government office. There was talk that he had emigrated to the colonies so he would have more opportunity to serve the British government. He too climbed from office to office, his purse growing fatter with each position.

Of importance to me these days, also, was a matter closer to home and hearth. Cotton had asked Molly to attend the holiday festivities. She had seemed agitated after attending the ball, but neither she nor Cotton would talk about the evening. So, it was a surprise to learn she agreed to a second engagement. But my heart is torn — as much as I love Cotton like a brother, Geoffrey is the match for my sister.

73

✦

I could always tell when Henry was scheming again. If he wasn't sneaking a bit of coin for a Faneuil Hall lottery ticket, he was swooning over sailors and their tales of whaling. Twice in as many weeks, I've caught him pilfering. He actually believes that he has a chance at winning the lottery!

Fall was the season for whaling expeditions, and men were setting up huts near the bay and watching for water spouts. Once a spotter sighted a spout, he would signal the crew to set out for the kill. Some crews would sail northward to hunt in the colder waters, a few bringing their families with for the entire hunting season. Inexplicably, my brother found this line of work to his liking.

"Listen, Eli!" Henry began to read aloud, nearly stumbling over the words in his excitement:

> A Number of Vessels are arrived from their Whaling Voyages, which in general has not been very successful.---One of them viz. Captain Clerk on Thursday Morning the 25th ult. discovering a Spermaceti Whale, near George's Banks, man'd his Boat, and gave chace to her, and she coming up with her Jaws against the Bow of the Boat struck it with such Violence that it threw a Son of the Captain's (who was forward ready with his Lance) a considerable Height from the Boat, and when he fell the Whale turned with her devouring Jaws opened, and caught him: he was heard to scream when she closed her Jaws, and part of his Body was seen out of the Mouth, when she turned, and went off.[14]

"What an adventure!" he finished.

"Didn't sound like such a good adventure for the man who was eaten."

"Can you imagine seeing that?"

"Yes, and I'd rather not."

Henry shook his head and stalked off to the kitchen.

I, too, shook my head, but I wondered at the extravagant notion of wanting to see a crew member eaten alive by one of those giant sea creatures.

---

[14] *Boston-Gazette, and Country Journal,* October 6, 1766.

November 1766

Molly Weston

"Have you heard?"

Mother had found a steady pace as she kneaded the bread dough. She dug the heels of her hands into the mass and pushed away, then folded the expanse back on itself and slapped it down onto the table. Then repeated the motions over and again.

"The 45's?"

"I can't imagine anyone defiling property like that," she exclaimed. Yet the gleam in her eye told me otherwise. She and I both knew about Eli and Henry spending their evenings marking windows and doors throughout the city with the infamous number. The publisher of the *North Briton*, John Wilkes, had been brought up on charges of libel against the King based on an article he supposedly had written but definitely published in Issue 45 of his periodical. The article wasn't signed, so many people felt the charges were a sham. Consequently, when he was jailed, people on both sides of the Atlantic rose up to support him.

"John Wilkes is an advocate of freedom in Britain, Mother. He is being imprisoned for speaking his mind. Hasn't that been our intent these last two years? Freedom to speak out against tyranny, freedom to run our own government, freedom to tax ourselves as we deem necessary?"

"Oh, yes, my child. But we mustn't allow ourselves to run wild again. The Council is still debating reparations for those damages to Hutchinson and Oliver. They lost nearly everything in those riots."

"Oh, humbug!"

"Language, dear."

I couldn't help but roll my eyes, but chose to change the subject nevertheless.

"Have you heard?" It was my turn to ask.

"Maybe."

I laughed. "Mr. Wilkes is so beloved in Boston that Nathaniel Barber named his son Wilkes."

"No! That is indeed humbug!"

"Honestly, Mother. All the women were talking about it as they came into Anna's shop yesterday. Nathaniel and Hepzibah baptized it Wilkes. Hepzibah had even pinned on a bow on its gown with the number 45. Now, that is a true protest for liberty."[15]

"How brazen! Poor little thing. He has no idea of the declaration he is making!"

---

[15] *Boston-Gazette, and Country Journal,* October 20, 1766.

January 1767

Hester Winslow

I had so enjoyed playing my part in the confrontation between Cotton and Lt. Canfield at the holiday celebration in July. The memory of Molly's cheeks turning red as beets when the two men exchanged words made me smile. To think that Molly could even consider herself a match for the son of a British lord! Such hubris!

And then a month later, Cyrus had been in The Three Lions at the time that those two had come to blows, and he had hurried home to tell me all the details. I couldn't help but giggle at hearing Cyrus describe the fisticuffs exchanged by Molly's two beaus. And beaus they were — the scuffle had confirmed my suspicions. Though I relished every detail of Cyrus's account, the most delectable was learning that not only had Molly seen the confrontation, but that she had been seen by others at the tavern.

Silly woman! She should never have set her marriage sights on an officer. After all, she is only the daughter of a tavern owner. Her ambition to marry above her sort is so obvious. Perhaps now she will understand her place and put an end to this ill-fated *affaire d'couer*.

I set aside thoughts of Molly as Cyrus and I began to dress for the night's concert. We tried to get out every day. If there wasn't a social event, we would at least walk the Common. The only way to learn what was happening in Boston was to see and be seen. And I planned on being seen, and learning, as much as possible. One never knows what information could be of assistance in the future.

I glanced once more at the advice from the front page of the *Gazette* to read about tonight's event:

For the Benefit of Mr. HARTLEY,

> Will be perform'd at CONCERT HALL,
> On the 15th Instant,
>
> A CONCERT
>
> Of Vocal and Instrumental Music, consisting of select Pieces by the most eminent Masters. To begin precisely at 6 o'clock. Tickets to be had at Concert-Hall, Brazen Head, Coffee House, Bunch of Grapes, and at Mr. *Hartley's* Lodgings next Door to Mr. *William Greenleaf's* the Bottom of Cornhill, at Half a Dollar each.[16]

"Cyrus! Come! It's time we left."

My husband draped the heavy woolen mantua around my shoulders and handed me a fox-lined muff. January's freezing temperatures would not dampen my resolve to attend the concert. We had come so far in my efforts to improve our social standing.

My beau and I had been happy to delay our marriage ceremony last year. It wasn't too difficult to join in such a small protest of the Stamp Act. Once I heard that a few engaged couples had chosen to not wed until they didn't have to purchase a stamp, Cyrus and I also postponed our nuptials. The response of the city caught us all by surprise. We had been feted around town as patriots, but more than being considered patriotic, I found that I enjoyed having all that attention lavished upon us. It made our engagement significant to others, and perhaps more importantly, it gave us influence. And I had determined not to let that influence fade.

As for Cyrus, well, I don't know that he paid much heed to being the object of the others' interest. It's not in his nature to pay attention to the subtlety and innuendo of social interactions. Even so,

---

[16] *Boston-Gazette, and Country Journal,* January 5, 1767.

no wife has ever had a husband as devoted to my wellbeing as my Cyrus. He will do whatever I want, and tonight, I want to step out and mingle with the upper sort. The city has been buzzing with activity and rumor — I can feel it — and I must be a part of it.

Geoffrey Canfield

Molly agreed to accompany me to the concert on Tuesday. It was billed as the first of seven choral concerts, one per week on Tuesday evenings. I had great hopes that tonight's social engagement would lead to a two-month protraction of choral events. A chance encounter, however, put that daydream at risk early in the evening.

"Molly! Molly!"

We both looked for the caller, but were caught unawares when we saw who spoke. Hester Winslow, the bona fide Mistress of Rumors.

Molly paled, but quickly rallied a smile and a warm greeting, albeit through a tightened jaw.

"Hester and Cyrus, it's good to see you again. I don't recall you being fan of music, Hester."

"Oh, no, you remember incorrectly. This evening is a perfect time for us to be out and about. Time to enjoy ourselves and the music, which you are doing as well." Her calculating eyes looked us up and down shrewdly, and both Molly and I detected a petty undertone to her clipped words.

Before the conversation degenerated, I sought to lessen the growing tension.

"Cyrus, it seems our ladies have neglected to introduce us properly, even though we have encountered one another previously." I reached out my hand and was relieved to see him smile. He thrust out his hand and pumped mine with enthusiasm. Obviously, he was as anxious as I to make a fresh start of the evening.

"I cannot believe we ran into her!" Molly was in a snit and wouldn't hear of changing the topic as we made our way home.

"She doesn't stop with the innuendoes! I can only imagine what she's saying to others. How can I show my face in public again?"

Her mood eventually turned my own humor black. Women and their concern for their reputation! Reputation was paramount in England, yet here in America, I couldn't reconcile their reasoning with my own. It was obvious, nevertheless, that the unkind Hester had dashed my wishes for a delightful start to our renewed courtship. I would need to right Molly's demeanor before I could begin my own plan to win her heart.

"Your friend, and I use that word lightly, treats everyone the same. From what I have seen of the woman, her efforts are a means of making herself feel more important than her sort. I daresay that most everyone will recognize her words for what they are — baseless rumors."

Molly sighed. "I hope you are right, Geoffrey. Words have the ability to cut and maim as deeply as any sword. Especially those of Hester."

Hester Winslow

Everyone of importance, and a few who had none, attended the concert. Doctors, lawyers, merchants, and their wives dressed in their finest frocks. Even members of the military attended. Across the room I saw Lt. Canfield, and once the crowd thinned a bit, I could see that he was accompanying Molly. That made me smile. Of course, we would make out way over to talk with them, but first, I would have to maneuver myself so that I could make the acquaintance of one of His Majesty's generals.

After catching the general's eye with a few coquettish moves of my fan, I shooed Cyrus away to look for some refreshment. Once I was alone, the portly gentleman in full military dress approached me carrying two cups.

"Ma'am, would you care for some wine?"

"Thank you, sir, but no. My husband is fetching us some." I lowered my eyes and spoke in my most demure voice.

"Perhaps this will slake your thirst until he returns." He smiled and proffered a glass.

He bowed towards me, although his rotundness allowed only a gentle tilt forward.

"General Emory Bridgewater of the British Royal Army. Now that you know my name, perhaps you won't be so hesitant to accept this offering of friendship."

I nodded my head and smiled.

"And I am Hester Winslow. Thank you for the wine."

As we chatted, I could feel myself more at ease with this man of position. When he revealed his command, I knew that tonight's social event had been a success. My newest acquaintance would open the window to exclusive views on Boston's activities, allowing me access to the upper sort. And perhaps give me some more insight to the mysterious Lt. Geoffrey Canfield.

February 1767

Eli Weston

Returning from the docks on Saturday evening, I found Geoffrey in what I considered our corner. A mug of ale sat untouched while he scowled into nothingness. In fact, I sat down and stared at him for several moments before his eyes focused and he saw me.

"Eli!"

I smiled at my friend and half-rose to clap him on the back.

"You're obviously thinking about something important."

Canfield sighed heavily and rubbed his face before answering.

"I fear we've been found out."

The words unleashed a cold breeze that blew through me.

"Well, you had best let it out so we know what or who our opponents are."

"Same as before. General Bridgewater."

"But how? Why now? It's been over a year."

"Would you move on so quickly? We destroyed a lot of his 'property.' All that black powder he would have turned into a sizeable nest egg."

"You're saying that he's been waiting, biding his time, before acting? And what can we expect from him?"

"I'm not sure."

"Then what are we talking about, Canfield!" I realized my voice was growing louder, so lowered it to a whisper. "It sounds as if you're worrying over nothing."

"Perhaps. Perhaps you're right. But if not, let's agree we must start preparing."

"Enough of the innuendo! Tell me why you're thinking like this. Surely we can work out a strategy to counter the brute."

"It was at the concert in January. I'm sure Molly has told you all about Hester."

I couldn't help but roll my eyes. Hester was all Molly was talking about lately.

"What she doesn't know, and I haven't told her precisely because of her concern about Hester, or better said, Hester's ability to spread rumors, is that I saw Hester talking to Bridgewater."

I exhaled sharply. That news truly deserved much attention. Equally important was that my friend hadn't mentioned this to me back in January.

"Still," I said. "It could be that Hester was flirting with the man. She is always looking to find a stepping stone for her and Cyrus to move up in society. Making the general an acquaintance would grant her access to a more affluent social circle."

"Don't you see, Eli? That is exactly the issue! Hester somehow intuited my feelings for Molly and has been turning that into a fount for rumors."

"How can it be a rumor if it's true? Most everyone in the tavern knows you have feelings for Molly."

Canfield continued as if he hadn't heard me. "If she is friendly with General Bridgewater, there's no telling what she will find out and then, with devious intention, begin to spread innuendo and nonsense. And, using what she hears from others as she spreads this gossip, she will surely unravel all that happened at the mill and who was involved."

I had to shake my head. Poor Geoffrey. I wasn't as downhearted at hearing this information as he was in telling me. In truth, Canfield sounded overly suspicious. But then, I trusted his judgment in other matters, so felt he deserved my support. How best to give it, however, I wasn't certain.

April 1767

Hester Winslow

We've had such a cold winter; I'm delighted to welcome Spring back to Boston. Cyrus has been working long hours and I feel quite bored with my duties as a wife. His salary has afforded us a house servant who manages the cooking and the more mundane chores like laundry. Now that the weather is more temperate, I can spend my days strolling along the Common, visiting friends for tea, and looking for opportunities to encounter General Bridgewater. Not seeing my newest acquaintance in the coffee house, and not seeing anyone of consequence with whom to converse, I collected a copy of the *Gazette* and began to read.

> Mary Phillips,
> Takes this Opportunity to inform the Public, That she has opened a School near Christ Church, and will teach young Ladies to Sew at *three Shillings* per Week, and Marking, Irish and Ten Stitch, and Embroidering; and will also take young Ladies to Board, or Half Board, at a reasonable Rate.[17]

Mary Phillips teaching stitchery! Her family must be experiencing an empty purse. But just thinking of Mary opening a school opened my mind to the possibility of opening one myself. My friends always said that my embroidery stitches were the smallest and most uniform, in short, the finest. Besides, more people know me

---

[17] *Boston Gazette and Country Journal*, April 7, 1767.

now— people of means who can pay for their daughters to be taught stitchery. If I were to charge less, say only two shillings a week, my classes would be full. And I would still have time to attend social events in the evening. Surely, Cyrus would let me keep the money. Oh, the dresses and other finery I could purchase with the income! The thought of new clothing excited me, and I began to plan my own school with visions of lace, feathers, and ribbons blending into the loveliest dress in my imagination.

"Mrs. Winslow!"

The call came from across the room, and I was so startled I nearly spilt tea all over the *Gazette*.

"Oh, General Bridgewater. How delightful to see you again," I feigned surprise for those seated around me, but the hefty military man knew our meetings were far from spontaneous.

The tall but corpulent man with the ruddy face was anything but pleasant looking, and sometimes I had to imagine I was gazing at some of the more handsome faces in town while we talked. Yet, he held a fascination for me. Whenever we met, he always had a new story to tell about the Royal Court, details about living in England, as well as humorous incidents and hair-raising experiences aboard ship. During our more recent encounters, he would talk about his work here in Boston. Ever since making his acquaintance, I had been sure to encounter him at the coffee house several times each week, biding my time to earn his confidence. After several weeks of these assignations, I was sure that he trusted me, and it was time to wheedle him into sharing information about Lt. Canfield.

May 1767

Molly Weston

"It's unbelievable!"

I squeezed the washing rag and scrubbed the iron kettle vigorously.

"Simply unbelievable!"

"What vexes you now?" Mother entered through the alley door and began to lay out her shopping purchases.

"Mary Phillips opened a stitchery school."

"Yes, I remember Anna mentioning that. She has always preferred Mary's delicate work for bespoke items. But why is Mary's school bothering you so?"

"Oh, it's not the school," I replied in a rather sarcastic tone. "Rather, it's that Hester has opened one on North Street, merely a few houses down from the old Hutchinson house. Mary opened her school across from Christ's Church, so Hester's location will be a draw for the young girls of the upper sort. Mary won't survive that competition."

"Mary's talent is well known in the city. She will do fine."

"I'm sure Hester only opened her stitchery school out of spite for Mary Phillips. Mary's needlework was always superior to the rest of us girls, and she always had an eye for color and design. Her talent is superior to Hester's, yet it looks as if Hester would have —"

"Molly, do not finish that thought! You have more than enough on your hands than to take on meddling in Mary's business."

"But it's Hester! She's becoming an intolerable pest! And Mary is too kind to put that mischief-maker in her place."

"And you're the one to do so?"

"Somebody needs to! It was bad when she was meddling in my affairs, but Mary doesn't deserve this treatment."

"I'd say that nobody does, Molly," Mother said softly. "But sometimes we need to turn the other cheek and let events take their own course."

Of course, Mother was right. Yet Hester's actions were more than being stubborn or contrary. I felt her circling around me, toying with my friends and dear ones, much as a hawk circles its prey. Either I was becoming too suspicious, or the woman was a true menace.

June 1767

Eli Weston

Ran-away the 21ˢᵗ Instant, from his Master *Stephen Harris,* Junr. a Servant Boy named *John Major,* 14 Years old, about 4 Feet high: Had on a light Cloath Pea Jacket, a blue Waistcoat, Leather Breeches, light rib'd Stockings, a blue mill'd cap, a Cotton & Linnen Shirt, and square Brass Buckles. Whoever takes up said Servant, and brings him to his Master, shall have *Two Dollars* Reward, and all necessary Charges paid by me, *S T E P H E N   H A R R I S,* JUNR.

    N. B. All Matters of Vessels and others are hereby caution'd against harbouring, concealing or carrying off said Servant, as they would avoid the Penalty of the Law.[18]

Another missing boy! What is going on these days? It seems that every other week a young lad disappears. Twelve years old was the youngest so far. Reading advices such as this one made me appreciate all the more Father's insistence of not apprenticing Paul and Henry. Apprentices had long terms of service as did indentured slaves, and I didn't relish the thought of being tied to one job and one master for such a long time. To avoid such a fate, I had volunteered to work at the docks when I was 15. Paul and Henry, however, were younger than me; they stayed at The Three Taverns and pretty much grew up into being tipplers and servers. Of course,

---

[18] *Boston-Gazette, and Country Journal,* June 1, 1767.

they did other tasks. Paul helped Father making ale and Henry was always volunteering to help with the shopping and errands. The boy did like to run!

I was beginning to think that Henry might be itching to try his hand at another way to make his mark in life. Late at night, as the tavern's customers head toward their homes, I often espy Henry chatting with a sailor or two about their lives at sea. He scours the paper for information about incoming and outgoing ships and is delighted to read of some of the adventures Edes and Gill publish. He'll have to polish his verbal skills, however, if he is to convince Father that he is able and strong enough to go to sea. It is a hard life, and one I think Mother would detest.

Molly Weston

Although the evening of the first concert had ended badly, Geoffrey hadn't been put off enough by Hester to avoid social situations where we might encounter her, and the next week, and every week after, we attended the town concerts. We quickly learned to dodge her and Cyrus by making a game of eluding the couple. We developed codes, both verbal and physical. Whoever first espied the woman would say, "the bird has nested," if she were coming, and "the bird has flown," if she were leaving. Should too many people be near, I would tap my fingers twice on his arm or he on my hand as we promenaded about the hall. At feeling the second tap, we would veer to the right or left, depending on Hester's location. With these artifices, we were able to avoid meeting her, and in some way, they afforded us an opportunity to share a secret. And it was this secret, I feel, that was the thread that began to tie us together once more.

After the seventh concert, Geoffrey devised more activities and entertainment for us. In June, on Harvard's Graduation Day, we spent most of the afternoon celebrating the baccalaureates. The entire city always turned out for this festive occasion honoring the young men who had completed their studies. Boston Common teemed with booths selling food and drink and others offering their wares. Anna always had a table where she would sell an assortment of her smaller habiliments such as fans, gloves, caps, and various odds and ends. Jane Eustis would compete, good-naturedly, of course, with her own feminine accoutrements. I found it peculiar that on this warm spring day she would have several fur muffs and tippets amongst her silks and satins with a sign advising that she would take cash. Had I thought more about the matter, I might have reasoned that the woman was in severe need of income.

As we browsed some of the items, I was taken aback by Geoffrey's attention to detail on one pair of gloves. He leaned over to inspect them closely and then gently picked one up and fingered its leather.

"Look how even these stitches are, Molly, and the leather is as soft as lamb's wool."

Anna and I looked at one another. Her eyebrows arched and I almost laughed out loud.

Geoffrey, however, didn't notice the exchange of nonverbal expressions. Instead, he had taken to looking at my hands and then at the gloves. Finally, he placed them back on the table.

"Shall we?" He offered me his arm, and I placed the elegant Irish lace handkerchief I had been admiring on top of the others. As we left Anna's booth, I turned my head and, from the corner of my eye, I saw her pick up the gloves he had been admiring and put them aside before greeting the next customers.

✦

Father had sent the last of The Three Lions' customers home, bolted the door, and turned in nearly an hour earlier. Geoffrey and I were still seated in the kitchen across from one another. We both sipped at cups of coffee long since gone tepid. A plate of cookies split the space between us, and from time to time, he would reach out for one of the buttery morsels. Although we hadn't spoken in many minutes, the silence was comfortable. More comfortable than it had been in a long time.

"Why did you do it, Molly?"

I looked up quizzically.

"Back at the mill. You kissed Cotton."

I blushed, but could no longer hold his gaze. My eyes dropped to my cup and I stared at the amber liquid I held in my hands. What had been a pleasant silence was growing increasingly uncomfortable. Mother had been right when she said I had hurt him.

93

"Molly, please look at me." He reached across the table and gently forced my chin upward with his forefinger. I squeezed my eyes shut so I wouldn't have to see him.

"I think I understand what happened, but we need to clear the air between us if we are to move forward . . . together."

He dropped his hand and I was free to lower my face. Tears splashed into my coffee, and I watched the ripples spread out and bounce off the cup's interior.

"I do owe you an apology," I said. The words finally had found their way out of my mouth, and as they did, I could feel an invisible burden lift from my chest. "I, I mean, it was a spur-of-the-moment thing. I was so relieved to see him, to see that he wasn't dead, and then I wasn't tied up any longer, and, well, I guess I felt happy to be alive."

Finally, I opened my eyes and looked directly into the blue eyes of my lieutenant.

"I would give anything to not have hurt you. But at the time, I didn't think, that is, I didn't realize you had seen . . . and later, well, so much time had passed."

"I believe you, Molly." At that, he rose, stretched out across the table, and found my lips with his.

July 1767

Eli Weston

Geoffrey was smiling ear to ear. I don't think I have ever seen anyone with such a pleased look on his face. He nodded at me, but instead of making his way over to our table, he detoured to the bar, poured himself an ale, and then wound through the tables and benches to where I was seated and straddled the bench to face me.

My raised eyebrows were enough of a question for him to begin to answer.

"Simple," he said. "She loves me." He took a big gulp of the cool ale.

I didn't think my eyebrows could go any higher, but they must have.

"Well, she will if she doesn't already."

"I assume we're talking about my sister?"

"Of course, my man!" He clapped me on the back. "It all worked. The concerts, Graduation Day . . ." He sighed and grinned some more.

"Good to hear, but I will caution you. This wasn't a ploy, was it? You do love her?"

He lowered his voice and leaned in. "Yes, I do love her! And I'd shout it from the rooftops were I able."

I looked him up and down, then smiled and nodded my acceptance. "Then, I'll give you my support however needed."

"Support for what?" asked Cotton.

Neither of us had seen him approach, and we weren't sure how much he had heard. Geoffrey fussed with his tankard, leaving me to reply.

I cleared my throat and hoped my voice wouldn't quaver. Instead, it sounded a bit too loud for the words that should have been spoken quietly. "For the next act of insurrection, of course!"

We were so worried about Cotton overhearing us talk about Molly that Cyrus's presence went completely unnoticed.

August 1767

Molly Weston

A copy of the July 27th *Evening-Post* lay on the table in front of me. We had heard of the New York Colony's refusal to quarter British soldiers, but it seemed that now Parliament was feeling a bit prickly. The newspaper had reprinted a new act that prohibited that colony's Assembly from governing. They weren't even allowed to meet! I sighed, wondering what more could Parliament do, when I saw that on the same day, the body had tried to pass a requirement that any person assuming an office in the government, whether in Britain or any colony, take a special oath.

> That the colonies and plantations in America are, and of right ought to be, subordinate unto, and dependant upon, the imperial Crown and Parliament of Great Britain; and that the King's Majesty, by & with the advice and consent of the lords spiritual and temporal, and commons of Great Britain, in parliament assembled had, hath, & of right ought to have, full power and authority to make laws & statutes, of sufficient force and validity, to bind the colonies, & people of America, subjects of the Crown of Great Britain, in all cases whatsoever.[19]

There's that phrase again, "in all cases whatsoever." Didn't anyone in Britain ever consider how that phrase would alienate us?

---

[19] *Boston Evening-Post,* July 27, 1767.

That last bit didn't pass, but knowing that the thought was in the minds of many in government didn't bode well for those of us across the ocean.

Mother interrupted my thoughts when she burst through the door waving a book in her hand.

"Molly! I've got it! Anna finished last night and has lent us her copy."

She plopped onto the kitchen bench to catch her breath, and I caught a glimpse of the cover.

"*Tristram Shandy?*"

"It's the ninth volume, the latest. Anna purchased a copy last month from John Mein when his latest shipment of books arrived. Of course, this is probably too trivial for you to read," she teased. "Maybe you'd prefer *Scipio and Berganza* by that Spanish author. John has copies of that, too, as well as *Marianne*."

"Cervantes? Is that what all the upper sort will be reading? Then, of course, I must read it as well," I teased back.

Of course, I had read all of the *Shandy* novels and thoroughly enjoyed the trials and tribulations of the protagonist. As for the Cervantes book, I wasn't sure that I was up to reading a novel that required me to interpret the author's meaning of a conversation between two dogs as they shared their reflections on mankind. We had enough philosophical battles of our own in Boston. I needed something lighter in topic and tone. I flipped through the pages of *Shandy*.

"When will you be done with it?" I asked.

Geoffrey Canfield

The papers are rife with advices for missing persons. Most notably, young men. Many times, these are working men — perhaps some are slaves or indentured servants — but regardless of their sort in life, the number of the missing men keeps rising. Yet again, I read in the *Evening-Post*

> Ran away from *Samuel Pearse* of *Plimouth*, an *Irish* indented Servant, about 5 Feet 6 inches high; had on when he went away, which was last Evening, a Felt Hat trimmed with green, short black hair, a greyish coloured thick Jacket, a red under Jacket, and a pair of Breeches of a redish colour. Whoever shall take up said Servant and return him to said *Pearse* at *Plimouth*, shall have *Six Dollars* Reward, and all necessary Charges paid
>
> by   Samuel Pearse.
>
> *N.B.* Said Runaway's Name is *James Brown*, hath had the Small Pox, and is something Pock broken.
>
> *Plimouth July 14, 1767.*[20]

The Royal Navy is not above kidnapping strapping young men to replenish the sailors who would desert once the ship is docked in port. The practice is abhorrent, yet the Crown barely looks askance at the manner in which the Navy conscripts its seamen. Of concern, however, is that Boston's citizens have taken note and it won't be long until they begin to assign guards to patrol the streets. I

---

[20] *Boston Evening-Post*, August 3, 1767.

fear that the Royal Navy may regret this decision should the hearty Bostonians interrupt the practice of impressment.

Eli Weston

Paul and Cotton were worn out. As much effort as I used to put into loading and unloading cargo from the ships moored at Long Wharf, they put into felling white pine in the forests outside of Boston. I looked at my younger brother and felt a bit of pride in the man he was becoming. These days, the lad who used to carry beer and rum swings an axe. Two years ago, he had stepped forward to help Cotton, Geoffrey, and me when we turned out all the patriots looking for Molly, but the boy had become a man.

It was mid-afternoon Sunday when Cotton waved me to the table they shared. The gobbet stew was nearly gone, but my youngest brother, Henry, quickly came by to replenish their bowls and bring me my own.

"We've run into a bit of a mess, Eli," Cotton said. "Looks as if Wentworth is prowling about again."

He was referring to John Wentworth, the surveyor general whose office required him to report individuals who didn't relinquish all the tallest and straightest pine for His Majesty's use in shipbuilding. These white pines were superior to anything on the European continent, and King George had decided that these forests were his to hew according to Britain's demand, regardless of quantity and without thought to our own need for lumber. Consequently, each tree was measured, felled, and set aside for shipping. Of late, however, Cotton and Paul had begun to stow some of those trees far from Wentworth's prying eyes. Not every stockpile had been hidden successfully, as I soon learned.

Cotton shoved a copy of the latest *Evening-Post* across the table and pointed to one of the advices:

Province of Massachusetts-   Boston, July 20.
Bay, Court of Vice Admiralty   1767

ALL PERSONS CLAIMING PROPERTY
in sundry Parcels of white pine Logs, Seized by *John
Wentworth,* Esq: Surveyor General of His Majesty's
Woods on the Continent of *America,* (for being cut
out of Trees growing in said Province contrary to
Law) at the several Places following, viz. at Pine-
Island 48, at Almsbury 319, at Bradford 4, at Andover
190, are hereby Notified to make their personal
Appearance at a Court of Vice-Admiralty, to be
holden at *Boston,* on the 5th Day of *August* next, at
nine o'Clock before Noon, to shew Cause (if any they
have) why the same Logs should not be decreed to
remain Forfeited, as prayed for by Information on file
in said Court.
        Per Curiam,   EZEQUIEL PRICE, D. Regr.[21]

"Have you worked any of these sites? I recognize only
Andover as a site you've logged."

American forests were being ritually culled. We Americans
were the ones to fell the trees, and at the same time, we experienced a
sense of ownership over them. But it was beginning to feel as if our
own property was being stolen and we were the ones carrying out the
theft. Cotton and Paul had enlisted other loggers to hold back some
of the best timber. They would fell the trees, and teams of horses

---

[21] *Boston Evening-Post,* August 3, 1767.

would drag the timber to caves and abandoned homesteads in an attempt to hide them from surveyor generals, such as Wentworth.

"Other than Andover, Cotton and I felled over at Pine Island only," Paul said. "You know, Wesley Smith's place."

I grimaced at the thought of Wes facing the Vice Admiralty court. Parliament had established several Vice-Admiralty courts in response to some of the grievances that aired during the Stamp Act riots up and down the coast. Previously, anyone prejudged guilty of an offense had only one recourse to contest the charge — travel to Halifax, Nova Scotia and appear in person. This was a costly trip, and those who had neither the time nor the funds to make such a journey paid a hefty fine and lived with their reputation forever marred. For each infraction of withholding timber, for example, one could be fined £100.

But with the repeal of the Stamp Act, Parliament had also determined that Boston would now be the seat of one of these Admiralty courts. For many of us, the new court seemed more of a punishment than an act of goodwill toward us Americans. It was the ever-present and watchful eye of a government bent on utilizing writs of assistance to line its coffers that chafed. Revenue officers would raid warehouses, shops, and even homes searching for items that had been smuggled or had somehow escaped the docks before the necessary custom fees had been paid. Several times a week, we would hear stories of merchants whose homes and warehouses had been raided without warning. The boycotts had severely divided the population. You were with the boycott or you weren't, and there were repercussions on both sides. Nobody knew who was pointing out potential offenders, which caused everyone to view one another with suspicion, which further divided the populace.

The printing of this advice alerted everyone that the revenue officers had expanded their reach to the forests and farms surrounding the city. Cotton, Paul, and the others would have to guard their illicit behavior more carefully.

"You must be more careful," I warned. "If Wentworth were to show up at Andover, you could all face punishment."

"We need a lookout. Someone fast and trustworthy." Cotton's eyes roamed the tavern and settled on Henry.

"No! He needs to stay out of this."

But my warning fell on deaf ears. Both Cotton and Paul were already waving Henry over.

Geoffrey Canfield

My father has taken to writing me on a regular basis. Each missive outlines a new program that Parliament is undertaking as a means to recuperate treasury funds they spent on a decades-long war. News in his latest letter, brought by ship via Nova Scotia, gave me pause.

"Parliament has established a new Board of Commissioners of the Customs, and it will be based in Boston," he wrote. "You'll remember William Burch and Henry Hulton, who have both been named to the Board. There are some Americans as well who were assigned to this duty, one from Boston."

He continued to inform me that although Lt. Governor Hutchison and Secretary Oliver should have been on the board, they would remain in their offices and their salaries would now be paid by the Crown, rather than by the Americans. He then took several paragraphs to summarize how new Articles of Commerce would tax the colonies even further. I could only shake my head wondering how my own ideas regarding government and its purpose had strayed from those of my father.

True to form, the following Monday, Edes published the features of Parliament's latest plan, which I read in the privacy of my room:

B O S T O N, August 10.

That the Board of Commissioners of the Customs was actually established, to consist of seven and a Salary of 500 l. each; and the Secretary and Receiver-General of the Board 300 l. each: —That Lieut. Governor Hutchinson and Mr. Secretary Oliver, would have been of the Board, but are provided for another Way, by Salaries to be paid them out of the Revenues raised on several Articles of Commerce, by which they, with all the Officers of the Crown, will be rendered independent of the People: —That the Rates on Lemmons, Wine, Fruit, &c. and also upon sheet, ground and flint Glass, Lead, Colours, Paper, &c. were not yet fix'd . . . —That nothing would be attempted by way of Internal Taxation of the Colonies.[22]

Unfortunately for Boston, Edes had left out some of the more exacting information on import duties, which father had generously annotated for me:

4 shillings a hundredweight on crown, plate, flint, and white glass; one shilling two pence a hundredweight on green glass; two shillings a hundredweight on paint and lead; flat rate of three pence a pound on teas of all grades; three pence to twelve shillings (thirty-six pence) a ream on 66 grades of paper. [23]

"Exchequer Townshend believes that these duties will bring in 20,000 pounds/year on tea while duties on glass, paint, lead, and paper will generate 17,000 pounds Sterling," he wrote.

"The only problem with this, dear father, is that now the American colonists have lost whatever influence they had over their government," I muttered.

Buttermilk mewed in agreement.

─────────────────

[22] *Boston Evening-Post*, August 10, 1767.
[23] *Boston Evening-Post*, August 10, 1767.

Eli Weston

Geoffrey joined me at the Green Dragon after the meeting of the Sons of Liberty had begun. Earlier in the day, Revere borrowed Henry's fleet feet to send word around town about some news from Parliament he had to share that would affect all of us.

Adams had the floor and was wailing about more taxation. His eloquent voice rose and fell to emphasize his points, but when he dropped to a near whisper, everyone learned forward to hear

> And, that the Address of the House of Commons to the King in behalf of the Gentlemen who suffer'd in the Colonies during the late Troubles, praying for some Recompence or peculiar Marks of the Royal Favor to them, was graciously answered by Assurances of his Majesty's Intention to Reward them for their Attachment to Government.[24]

The roar from his listeners was deafening. Hutchison and Oliver would be receiving even more money from Boston taxpayers in addition to the payment from the Crown for their office. The Sons were not pleased.

"It may be necessary to recompense the men for their losses," Geoffrey murmured, "but making an announcement in this manner only incites the people more."

He pulled me over to a corner and leaned in closely.

"Have you noticed anyone following you lately?"

---

[24] *Boston Evening-Post*, August 10, 1767. This is the first hint of the Townshend Acts that included the Revenue Act.

Though I found the idea pure folly, I could see that Geoffrey was serious.

"A red coat trailing me? But why me? Our activities haven't been so drastic that I would merit being followed."

"I'm pretty sure it's not the British who are spying on us, Eli. As I approached the tavern, I saw Cyrus Winslow skulking across the street."

"That milksop wouldn't recognize any mischievous behavior if he stumbled into the middle of it."

"Perhaps not, but all he need do is report what he sees to his wife. Hester will sort through the grist and find the most promising kernels to promote her latest gossip."

Geoffrey was cocksure that Winslow was spying, but the idea couldn't find purchase in my mind. "But again, why? What would be the purpose? He's an American. At least he acted like a patriot during the Stamp Act protests."

"And yet he lurks in the shadows across from the Green Dragon while the Sons of Liberty are meeting. If he is such a patriot, why isn't he here?"

"Maybe he's afraid of taking a public stance? You've seen how Hester wears the breeches in that union."

"Then you're suggesting that she's a Royalist? That would only support my reasoning of his following you, me, all of us!"

"Geoffrey, if you're correct, then he, she, whoever, will have deduced that you're walking a treasonous path."

My friend walked over to a window and peered out through a knothole in the slatted shutters.

"Hmm. Doesn't seem to be there now."

Trying not to think the worst, I offered up a meek excuse. "Perhaps it was a coincidence that you both happened to be in the vicinity of the Green Dragon."

Geoffrey gave me a sideways glance and shrugged. "Maybe."

His tone, however, told me that he didn't believe a word I said.

September 1767

Eli Weston

Boston is in an uproar.

First, Ben Edes published a letter in his broadsheet that set tongues a-wagging with rumors:

> B O S T O N, September 7
> A letter of the 13th of June, from a Gentleman in London to his Friend in Boston, says, "It is Lord Mansfield's Opinion, that the Authors of the Riots and seditious Pieces in America, should be sent for to England, and there tried for Treason."[25]

With Governor Bernard pushing the Massachusetts Assembly to determine who caused the damage two years ago August, the notice in August that more taxes were to be levied, and now this small advice . . . the three had the effect of a lit match on kindling. Even I was a bit nervous to think of my part in the riots. Although I had abandoned the crowds after reaching Oliver's office, it was no secret that I had been at the front of the march beginning at Liberty Tree.

But Governor Bernard was also pushing the town to repay Lt. Governor Hutchinson and Andrew Oliver for the damage to their homes during those two weeks of riots. Estimates on Hutchinson's house alone ran to more than £2,300. Granted, rioters had thoroughly sacked and burned the structure, but to exact payment

---

[25] *Boston-Gazette, and Country Journal,* September 28, 1767.

from citizens who struggled to feed their families and pay their own taxes! All in all, the tension in the air was building.

Immediately upon the announcement of its formation, the new Board of Customs began to strictly enforce customs regulations. John Hancock must have known of the board's plans — he was among several of Boston's most respected citizens who refused to attend the welcoming ceremony. Of course, a short while earlier, he had purchased the second largest dock on the harbor where he moored the *Lydia*, his ship that regularly sailed to the West Indies to smuggle molasses and wine, among other necessaries. The dock gave him a location for launching a new shipbuilding business, which put him into direct competition with the Crown for timber. This new endeavor had established him as a favorite among the carpenters, joiners, rope makers, and coopers whose economic woes were being eased. With his new business, Hancock had raised his own army of laborers who would join him, if necessary, against any threat.

The colony's smaller traders were struggling to pay the necessary duties to collect the goods they had been commissioned to acquire. Overseas merchants were being taxed as well, but they were passing the extra fees to their clients. As always, the final cost would be paid by the last consumer.

In addition, the customs officials-turned-revenue officers had expanded their operations. Of late, the King's men were busy scavenging the forests to strengthen the Royal Navy while others were raiding homes and shops for illegal goods. The officials were levying fines on merchants, shopkeepers, importers, and nearly anyone who may require goods brought in by ship. It was time for the Sons of Liberty to launch a counterattack.

I was deep in thought when Thomas Young met up with me as I left The Three Lions. The newest of Boston's medical professionals had quickly installed himself as a hard-working patriot of the Committee of Correspondence and the Sons of Liberty. While

111

in New York, the doctor had worked against the Stamp Act and helped to establish that city's Sons of Liberty. Even though he served as John Adams's personal physician, I really had no knowledge of why he had uprooted his wife and two children from Albany to move east. Nevertheless, I was grateful to have someone as educated and well-spoken molding the image of both groups.

"North End Caucus has its hands full."

"How so?"

"The sailors are back at it."

"I've seen more of them at the docks. Hard to keep from stepping on them down on Long Wharf."

"Have you heard about the scraps happening over at the rope works? The sheriff is wanting to charge the brawlers. Doesn't seem right."

I nodded but remained quiet while we continued to walk. Young was referring to yet another hardship we Americans were enduring — the high number of sailors who had been swarming off newly docked ships and taking over jobs from local men. Sailors who had several months to spend on our shores before shipping back to Europe were being paid double — once for their work at sea and now for a job on land. Sailors were using their skillset to force themselves into the manufactory and repair of ships and rigging. The rope works were full of the tars.

Our families were suffering enough with high inflation, but to take our jobs! Men and boys old enough to work roamed the streets and the docks looking for employment. Jobs were scarce enough when we competed with one another, but the idea that merchants and artisans would pay sailors less rather than employ their neighbors at a fair wage was worse than salt in a wound — it was a kick to the stomach. Those employers were showing their true colors, and their backs were red as the boiled lobsters they hired.

Young chuckled bitterly. "Parliament 'declares' that Americans are 'subordinate unto and dependent upon the imperial crown,' and too many are taking that to mean any man wearing the royal uniform is lord and master over us. Perhaps another touch of anarchy is in order."

"What's our first step?"

✦

William Molineux took the floor once the meeting was called to order. The upstairs room at the Green Dragon was filled with an assortment of laborers, shopkeepers, and merchants. Sam Adams was hunkered in a corner with Paul Revere; Dr. Warren and John Hancock sat nearer the front and off to the left of Molineux. Pipe smoke thick as spring fog floated at eye level, painting everyone with a grayish tinge. As I listened to William, it became obvious that he and Sam had discussed the issue about jobs thoroughly.

"How many of you came to work today to find that a lobster back had taken your job?"

"Hear! Hear!"

"There isn't enough work in the city to hire someone who's planning to leave as soon as his ship sails! We must insist that our countrymen hire Americans. There's only one way to let the British know that we will not abide this behavior! We march on the perpetrators!"

The room erupted with huzzahs and clapping. I looked at Thomas, who smiled knowingly and nodded his head. In my mind, what I was seeing came into focus. Molineux worked with the middling sort, that is, the merchants and artisans. Young, as a physician, work with the city's better sort. And Adams, he with the silvered tongue, brought everyone together. A holy trinity of masterminds for Boston's latest season of unrest.

✦

My youngest brother Henry had begged me to come, so I made sure we smudged our faces with ashes from the kitchen's hearth before sneaking out into Gallops Alley. We walked in silence along Fish Street toward the harbor. Molineux had called out a brigade of 8 to meet up at the customs house.

One by one, other brigade members joined us on the street. Marching two abreast, our faces blackened by soot, we made a formidable group. A few men held cudgels for protection, but I made sure that neither Henry or I did. I preferred to fight with my fists, and as for Henry, well, I wanted him to flee should a skirmish break out — his speed would protect him. Everyone, however, had either a knife, awl, or an adze.

"Over here!"

Molineux had moved ahead to scout the area. The evening was calm, nary a lobster back in sight. Soldiers and tars had already found a tavern bench to warm for the evening.

"Remember, etch in the number 45 on the lintel, jamb, or window sash for every building along the wharf."

"Make it big, fellas!" I yelled. "Make sure they know that our support is behind John Wilkes. Wilkes and Liberty!"

"Wilkes and Liberty!"

"Wilkes and Liberty!"

We carved, whittled, and gouged our way along the wharf for several hours before taking our writing instruments and heading home. In the morning, the British would know that we supported freedom, in America as well as Britain, above all else.

Geoffrey Canfield

I pulled out the suede leather gloves I had purchased from Anna Adams and stroked the nap. My finger traced the light brown leather making it darker, and the back stroke returned it to a lighter color. Anna had assured me that these would fit Molly's hands. At the same time, I purchased the lacy handkerchief my beloved had been admiring. Anna, too, had assured me that the one in my hands was the same. Now that the evenings brought in cooler temperatures, and the sea breeze was crisper than before, the time had come to present her with these tokens of affection.

I met up with Molly as she left Anna's shop for the day.

For a few minutes, I watched her from a few paces behind. She stopped periodically to peer into a shop window, and I slowed my gait to match hers. This young woman walked with purpose, yet she didn't feel the need to rush. She stood straight and proud but lacked the pretense that sprang forth from Hester much like soot from a chimney. Molly made me smile, and I lengthened my strides to overtake her.

"Miss, may I accompany you?"

"Oh! Geoffrey, you know that you may!" And she slipped her hand into the crook of my elbow and rested it easily.

"Where shall we walk today?"

"It's too chilly to go near the harbor. Shall we stroll toward the north?"

As we walked toward Old North Church, my free arm fumbled in my pocket to loosen the handkerchief from the package.

"What are you doing? Do you need to use both hands?" She stopped and looked at me quizzically.

"No, it's nothing."

She turned and again rested her hand in my elbow.

I could feel the lace with my fingers, and worked to ease the item from the paper wrapping. My forefinger and thumb plucked the handkerchief and balled it up in my hand. Slowly, I pulled my hand out of my pocket and released the handkerchief so it would fall to the ground.

"Oh, look!"

Molly saw the white lace flutter to the ground. "Oh, it will get dirty!"

She snatched it up and gently shook it to release the bit of dust it had already acquired.

"Such a pretty thing." She looked at it closely, and suddenly she looked at me with surprise in her eyes.

"This is the handkerchief!"

I laughed and gave her a quick hug. "Yes, it is the very same."

"Geoffrey, it is so lovely. Is it for me?"

I nodded, smiling ear to ear. My heart was smiling as well.

She clutched it to her breast. "I shall always treasure it."

"Then perhaps you will treasure these as much." I reached into my pocket and pulled out the gloves. "I've been assured they will fit."

"You and Anna have been in league!"

"Yes, miss. We are both guilty of colluding to make you happy."

"And you have! These are lovely gifts. Perhaps too lovely and too expensive to accept."

"Don't return them!" I pleaded. "Why would you?"

"They have a meaning more than their value, you know. You do know, don't you?"

Relieved, I smiled once again and nodded. "Yes, Molly, I am aware of what a gift such as this means. These items were chosen specifically for you precisely because of that meaning."

116

I stopped smiling so she would acknowledge the sincerity of my words. "These gloves and this handkerchief are my gifts to you, my promise to you."

When my voice broke, so did she, and I kissed her lips lightly to seal that pledge.

Eli Weston

Paul and Cotton are back in the city, and Cotton is sniffing around The Three Lions looking for Molly. Every time he comes in, he either sits and moons over her tawny hair or blue eyes, or he wanders around the great room and into the kitchen looking to see where she might be. Truly he is love-struck, for I have never seen him like this. If he weren't so besotted by my sister, I'd box him around the ears to sober him up. Then we could have a conversation again, or even play some dice! Instead, like a good friend, I sit and listen to his sentimental woes and romantic plots to win her heart. Unlike a good friend, as I listen to his amorous drivel, my mind debates whether to tell him about Geoffrey.

Because he's been in the forests, Cotton hasn't seen my British friend escorting Molly to the concerts and market days. If I were to be realistic, Geoffrey and Molly have rekindled that budding romance and nurtured it into a flourishing bloom. Cotton hasn't a chance with my sister, although there was a time when we were younger that I wouldn't have pictured her with anyone else. These days, however, events have thrown two unlikely souls together, and they are a match.

"I never see her anymore, Eli."

"What's that?" Cotton's remark broke into my thoughts about Geoffrey and Molly, and I might have blushed a bit as if I had been caught sneaking an extra cooky from mother's tray.

The time was now. I couldn't let him continue on in his fanciful dreams.

"Cotton, let's take a walk."

✦

Boston Common, fifty acres of grass and trees, home to Liberty Tree was used frequently as a grazing lea for cattle (and a few pigs). That afternoon, the livestock lazily munched on the last of summer's green grass and watched Cotton and me as we circled the Common four times. First, he yelled at me for daring to dispute his feelings. Then he stomped and brandished his fists at an imaginary Geoffrey. That monologue gave way to one in which he berated the British in general, and the King in particular, for endangering his chance at love by leaving a standing army in America. By our fourth circuit, his voice became subdued, most likely from overexertion on his previous rants, and he resigned himself to the truth. Head down, hands in pockets, feet shuffling the dry dirt, he walked alongside me back to the tavern.

Geoffrey Canfield

One of the benefits of Paul and Cotton working in the forest is not having to run into Molly's false suitor on a regular basis. In fact, I hadn't seen the fellow in months till today.

My troops and I had come off duty that evening when I glimpsed Cotton's familiar blonde mane bobbing as he huddled with Eli excitedly talking about a topic dear to his heart. *Has to be about Molly.*

"Let's see about some supper, lads," I slapped the back of my closest underling and propelled him toward the kitchen. I knew I'd feel better if I put distance between Cotton and me, even if it seemed he hadn't seen us.

Later that evening, Eli let me in on the conversation he had with Cotton.

"That wasn't a conversation for you to have."

"Maybe not, but he is an old friend. I could no longer abide his fanciful dreams of a future with a girl who doesn't share that interest."

I picked up my boot and a stiff brush and vigorously scrubbed the day's dust and caked-on mud from the footwear.

Eli watched me for a bit and suddenly stood when it seemed I wasn't going to reply.

I looked up at my tall friend and sighed.

"You've been placed in a tight spot, Eli. I apologize for that. It can't have been easy to balance my interests with those of Molly and then weigh those of Cotton as well."

I stood and shook his hand. "Thanks for your support."

✦

The next morning, I rose to Buttermilk nuzzling my ear. I guess someone was interested in heading out to hunt down her breakfast. Some months back, I'm not sure just when, Buttermilk had adopted me and now I was her chief caretaker. So, after my ablutions, she followed me to the kitchen where I opened the door for her. Now that she was taken care of, I turned to foraging for my own morning meal as both Molly and her mother were inconveniently absent.

The kitchen door slammed against the wall as Cotton stepped in. His brash entry took me by surprise, especially as he was typically well-mannered and mindful of his surroundings. This morning, however, his disheveled appearance and red-rimmed eyes were but two symptoms of his apoplectic nature.

"Where's Molly? I have to talk to Molly." His head moved side to side as his eyes scanned the room. They passed over me, but didn't pause. It was as if he hadn't recognized me.

Eli had assured me that Cotton had come to terms with the relationship Molly and I had formed, but those actions didn't belong to someone who had heard, and more importantly, accepted such news peacefully.

Not seeing anyone (me included), he then raced into the great room. I followed apace, not knowing who he might encounter in his agitated state.

I heard him before I saw what was happening. Cotton had run into Molly's father, Jonathan.

"Cotton. Good grief, man, get hold of yourself!"

"It's, it's . . . I . . .oh, I don't know!"

Eli's friend had found a bench and now held his head in his hands. Jonathan was seated beside him and was patting him on the back in a gentle manner.

121

I backed out of the room before they saw me. If Jonathan could comfort the rejected suitor . . . well, it would be better received than anything I could say to that tormented soul.

October 1767

Molly Weston

Mother's waking hours are even busier these days, but if ever they had been more leisurely, I couldn't say. For several weeks now, Reverend Mayhew's replacement, Simeon Howard, has been encouraging his female congregants to take action of their own making. His favorite theme was to attain personal holiness through civil and religious freedom. Sermons that once encouraged good deeds toward our fellow man now urged us to deeds that would exclude those who lived across the ocean. Every congregant was obligated to participate to the best of his ability. Our loyalties are to God, family, and America. Our duty is to uphold our country. The reverend would always close the service with a benediction — noticeably absent were the words beseeching blessings on the King and his Parliament.

On Sunday instant, Reverend Howard laid out a plan utilizing the skills of the fairest amongst us. Upon hearing his proposal, I sensed a difference in mother's bearing. She was sitting straighter, her eyes gazing beyond the walls of the sanctuary. I nudged her with my elbow so that she would bow her head in prayer, but even then, her spirit was honing an idea dissimilar from the prayers intoned by our spiritual leader.

Walking home, I asked what preoccupied her.

"Molly, for two years I have watched you work with your brothers and I've wanted to help."

"But you do help. You keep us fed, and when nosy Tories start looking too closely, you turn them in another direction. That is invaluable to us!" I felt as if I were the parent helping to guide my daughter in her decision-making process.

She sighed, and I detected a hint of desperation.

"And yet you are the ones always in peril. I have been feeling that I could do more, and now I know that I can."

My eyes were focused on the walkway that was generally uneven and occasionally pitted with small-to-large holes. I stole a glance upward and waited for her to continue.

"I will start the ladies' spinning circle."

I stopped and stood upright to look her in the eyes. My mother hadn't spun cloth in years. She had learned to spin at her mother's knee, and she dutifully taught me when I was a girl. But as she and father expanded the tavern to a publick house and an inn, there was little time for many of the domestic tasks. If we didn't purchase a new pair of breeches or a petticoat from Anna's shop, we at least purchased the yardage to sew the needed item. But spinning? That was such a laborious chore!

We only ever spun wool, but many of our neighbors had spun flax into linen that would then be woven into yard goods for shirts, shifts, and scarves, and the finest weaves were dedicated to stockings. I thought back to the days when mother showed me how to manipulate the treadle at a constant speed so the wheel spun the thread to a consistent thickness. I looked at my hands and suddenly wished for those days when the wool's lanolin would coat my hands, making the skin soft and pliable. *Did we even still have a wheel?*

The following morning, I couldn't believe my eyes. What happenstance that homespun clothes were the main interest of Reverend Howard and my mother, for now even the *Boston Evening-Post*[26] had published that Peter Templeman, secretary to the Society for Encouraging Arts and Sciences, would give instructions on growing and harvesting hemp to be used in lieu of flax for linen. *How many women are resolute in their efforts to make and wear homespun? Resolute*

---

[26] *Boston Evening-Post*, August 3, 1767.

enough to sow a field, tend the crop, and then harvest it in addition to spinning and weaving? That seemed a bit much to ask, but when I considered how many more tasks mother and I had added to our daily activities since last August, perhaps it wasn't such a fantastic idea after all.

✦

Mother would not be hindered in her efforts. She quickly recruited Anna, and the two of them visited friends and neighbors, cajoling women under the guise of friendship to participate in their spinning circle. Reverend Howard had offered the church for the women to use as their makeshift manufactory, but Anna preferred the women set up in her shop.

Come the following Monday morning, five women had joined the two in spinning. By Friday, they numbered eight. Other spinning circles formed throughout the city, and soon we could see girls and women carrying their wheels to the locale of their spinning circle. It amused the men to see women hoisting their wheels on their shoulders through the streets, but none dared to venture a negative comment.

Anna's shop was now filled with spinners, each one wanting to contribute to the nonimportation and non-consumption effort. She tasked me with finding others who would weave our thread into cloth, and later to find merchants and shopkeepers who would sell our yard goods. It was easier to find weavers than merchants. Up and down King Street, Fish Street, and Queene Street I went in and out of shops. We were more trusting than hopeful that the shops would sell our fabric. Didn't we share a goal to cripple the British economy by not importing and not purchasing European products? Our earlier boycott of imported goods was a successful effort in helping to get the Stamp Act repealed. Now, we needed to discipline ourselves once again to prove to Parliament that America would not bow down to their latest attempts at taxation.

125

After several afternoons of visits, however, it became obvious to me that no merchants or shops were seeking fabric to sell. Although these merchants had signed the non-importation agreement, they had ample supplies of European yardage in store and none were inclined to purchase more, even if the cause were true.

One shopkeeper peeved me more than most. Jane Eustis. She had not yet signed the non-importation agreement, and she continued to sell European goods. In addition, she was audacious enough to continue publishing advices in the newspaper, which galled me. I threw the broadsheet across the kitchen one October morning, thoroughly disgusted by seeing yet another advice.

Jane Eustis

Has just imported from *LONDON*, in the Captains *Scott, Bruce* and *Deverson*, a large Assortment of Goods, which she will sell very cheap for Cash, *viz.*

FUR Muffs and Tippets, fur trimmings, Bath beaver coating, serges, scarlet cloth, breeches patterns, white flannel and baize, sballoons, camblets, cambleteens, stript camblets, duroys, tammies, durants, callimancoes, black & ell russell, coloured crapes, barleycorns, Irish camblets, daykes, Scotch plaid, brocades, stript and flower'd silks, (some of the stript as low as 46s. O.T. a yard) brown and black padusoy; green, pink, grey and brown ducapes; green, white, pink, buff, brown and grey mantuas; rich white sattin, cloth-colour ditto, 1/4 & 1/2 ell figured sattins, pelong sattins, capuchine silks, taffaties, Persians . . .[27]

---

[27] *Boston-Gazette, and Country Journal*, October 28, 1768.

126

Even though Jane hadn't signed the nonimportation agreement, Anna worried that Jane would be coerced into signing by some of the more vehement members of the Body of the People. After the Body had voted to pass the Letter of Nonimportation, more and more frequently, members would invite themselves into a merchant's shop to convince the latter to sign the agreement. Rumors flew around the tavern about how some of those men used force to get those signatures. I shuddered to think of what kind of threats non-signing merchants might endure. I hoped that these members would not be physically violent with the women shopkeepers.

There were many women, however, and I was one, who were determined to get those women shopkeepers to sign the nonimportation agreement. I took it upon myself to stop in to visit with her day after day, but each time would find her with customers. She would glance at me and turn back to her customers. As I didn't have time to wait for her attentions, I would leave. Finally, one afternoon I was able to get her alone and she signed, but she continued to sell imported goods. Today, I needed to impress upon her the value of her cooperation.

"Molly, I have all this merchandise."

"But Jane, everyone must participate. The strength of the boycott is in the number of participants."

"Molly, you don't understand. I must earn a living. This shop is all I have since . . . well, since I've been alone."

Jane's stubbornness tried my patience, but when my eyes met hers, I saw the pain that had become her constant companion. I relented and embraced the small woman, a conciliatory gesture for my harsh tone of earlier.

Anna, mother, and I all wanted Jane to work with us and the Daughters of Liberty, but I no longer had much of a heart to talk her into pulling her imports from sale. Jane's husband had left her for a younger woman several years earlier, and her shop was the only way for her to earn a living. Jane's health had even suffered from the humiliation of that event. She had become withdrawn and frail, and a persistent cough interrupted her speech. I wanted her to be strong-willed and stand with the other Daughters, but I could no longer fault her for selling the European goods she already had in warehouse. My emotions swayed back and forth, from righteous anger at Jane's hampering of our efforts to outrage at the position in society into which she had landed through no fault of her own.

"I'd probably do away with Geoffrey if he were to take up with a jill," I muttered.

Opposition to the Townshend Act was not as strong as it had been to the Stamp Act in 1765. Two years after the riots, we were still dealing Loyalists tracking down rioters to ship them to England for trial. The governor was working to make reparations to Hutchison and Oliver for their losses, and in general, people didn't seem to mind the new taxes. It was as if they felt that because these new taxes weren't as onerous as those in the Stamp Act, there was no reason to support a boycott.

I still had to make a few more visits to other merchants before returning to Anna's shop. Peter Oliver had been talking around town about how entertaining it was that all the lower sort was signing the agreement. His attitude was but one reason why so many of us were signing — his words belittled the women who cleaned his house, cooked his meals, and did his laundry. Every last citizen of Boston needed to comply with the agreement, and I intended to see that each person signed.

Eli Weston

Henry is beside himself. I've been watching him the last two weeks, and he's almost giddy. I finally cornered him during a lull at the tavern, and I couldn't believe what he had to tell me.

"It's been almost a year, but I've finally saved up nearly enough money to buy my lottery ticket. The tickets are dear, four dollars each!"

"You still think that you can win? Games of chance are aptly named — you would need more than a stroke of luck to make any money — and if that's how you are playing, then you as well as the lottery organizers are nothing more than cheats." I shook my head at his naïveté.

"You and Father never believe that anything good can happen."

"Because for good to happen, you must work toward the desired end. The means do not justify the end, rather, the means ensure the justifiable end."

"It's not a foolhardy game, Eli. For the four dollars spent on a ticket, I could win two thousand! And this Faneuil Hall Lottery, Letter F[28], promises to be the best ever. They're offering more prizes, so even if I win the smallest prize, it will have brought in two dollars more than the ticket price. Even the odds are good — 728 prizes out of only 2,250 tickets sold. Surely you and Father would approve of those odds."

"The Three Lions needs the money," he continued. "You'll change your mind when you see me win."

------

[28] *Boston-Gazette, and Country Journal*, October 12, 1767.

As he turned back toward the rum spigot, I could hear him muster his positive outlook chanting, "I *will* win!"

I chuckled and picked up a copy of the *Gazette* only to read that merchant sailors, or in this case, smugglers, had been working hard to impress men into maritime service. Captain Jeremiah Morgan had even outfitted his dinghy with enough armament to ensure he left with the men he came to kidnap. This foray, however, was unsuccessful.

> By the Virginia Gazette, of the first Instant (Oct 1), it appears that Captain Morgan, of the Hornet Sloop of War, concerted a bloody riotous Plan, to impress Seamen, at Norfolk, for which Purpose, his Tender was equipped with Guns and Men, and under Cover of the Night said Morgan landed at a publick Wharff, having first made proper Dispositions either for an Attack or Retreat, then went to a Tavern, and took a cheerful Glass, after which they went to work, and took every Person they met with, and knocked all down that resisted; and dragged them on board the Tender; but the Town soon took the Alarm, and being headed by Paul Loyal, Esq; a Magistrate, they endeavoured to convince Capt. Morgan of his Error, and being deaf to all they said he ordered the People in the Tender to fire on the Inhabitants, but they refused to obey their Commanders Order, and he was soon obliged to fly, leaving some of the Hornets behind, who were sent to Goal, but were afterwards released.[29]

---

[29] *Boston-Gazette, and Country Journal*, October 26, 1767.

It wasn't only the Royal Navy we had to be careful of these days. I looked over at Henry bustling about the tavern. *Be careful, brother*, I silently prayed.

Geoffrey Canfield

More young men have gone missing. Now the advices are announcing rewards for their return. The latest fellow, an apprentice from Lynn, went missing on the 22nd.

> RAN-away from the Subscriber
> on the 20th Instant, an Apprentice Lad, named *William Flint*, in his 18th
> Year, of a middling Stature, light complection, blue Eyes, something full Mouth'd, a little round-shoulder'd, short sandy Hair, if not cut off.
> Whoever takes up and secure said Servant, so that his Master may have him again, shall have FOUR DOLLARS Reward, and all necessary Charges, paid,
> by   YOUNG FLINT
> All Masters of Vessels, and others, are hereby caution'd against harbouring, concealing or carrying of said Servant on Penalty of the Law.[30]

On Penalty of Law! I scoffed at the absurdity of the statement. Had anyone been paying attention to the law, these young men wouldn't be missing. None of the captains of merchant vessels nor those of the Royal Navy ever had any intention of obeying the colony's rule of law.

Life with his master had to have been particularly cruel and barbarous if Flint had to escape. Apprentices were routinely maltreated and underpaid, if paid at all. Hence, it was even more

---

[30] *Boston-Gazette, and Country Journal*, October 26, 1767.

preposterous that young Mister Flint would have to pay the reward for his return.

I hated to think of the conditions the lad would be facing if rather than simply running away, he had been kidnapped and impressed by the navy. Weeks spent at sea, in weather both good and foul, food not fit for a pig's consumption, and the longest and most grueling of work days were things no man should ever have to endure.

I bowed my head. "God keep him safe."

Eli Weston

Sam Adams had been talking with James Otis for days now, and when he crossed the threshold of The Three Lions that Monday, I knew that he had news to share.

"Eli! Come sit with me!" Adams hollered across the room.

I drew two mugs of ale as he plopped down onto a bench and began to pull all sorts of papers from his waistcoat. Once the ale reached his elbow, he dropped the papers and greedily gulped down some of the golden brew.

"Eli, we've done it! This will get their attention!"

He wiped his mouth on his sleeve and flattened out several sheets of paper replete with Otis's ornate penmanship.

"We'll present this at the town meeting on Wednesday night, the 28th."

The lawyer sorted through the papers and selected a letter.

"I received this letter only yesterday, but it will give Boston's Body of the People the incentive it needs to pursue the nonimportation and non-consumption agreements."

He shoved the letter into my hands, and as I scanned the pages, he shuffled through the mass of papers until he found what he wanted.

"As moderator of the meeting on Wednesday, Otis will make several proposals. What say you?"

He grabbed the letter and replaced it with another page filled with inky script.

> Whereas the excessive Use of foreign Superfluities in the chief Cause of the present distressed State of this Town, as it is thereby drained of its Money; which Misfortune is likely to be increased by Means of the late additional Burthens and Impositions on the

Trade of the Province, which threaten the Country with Poverty and Ruin . . .[31]

I looked up and eyed the lawyer with suspicion.

He smiled coyly. "We will propose to manufacture everything we presently import from Britain. And what we cannot manufacture, we will not consume. I've enumerated some of the items for the list."

The list was a bit like Sam Adams, long and disorganized. I could imagine him sitting at his desk writing down items as they occurred to him: Clothing was listed next to furniture, and then accessories followed spices. The assortment made me dizzy to contemplate:

> Loaf Sugar, Cordage, Anchors, Coaches, Chases and Carriages of all Sorts, Horse Furniture, Men and Womens Hatts, Mens and Womens Apparel ready made, Houshold Furniture, Gloves, Mens and Womens Shoes, Sole-Leather, Sheathing and Deck Nails, Gold and Silver and Thread Lace of all Sorts, Gold and Silver Buttons, Wrought Plate of all Sorts, Diamond, Stone, and Paste Ware, Snuff, Mustard, Clocks and Watches, Silversmiths and Jewellers Ware, Broad Cloths that cost about 10s. per Yard, Muffs Furrs and Tippets . . . [32]

"Sam, you've listed nearly everything. Surely we can't manufacture all of these items here."

---

[31] *Boston-Gazette and Country Journal,* November 2, 1767.
[32] *Boston-Gazette, and Country Journal,* November 2, 1767.

"Pshaw, Eli! Of course, we can! Even if we can't, isn't it worth trying another boycott to energize the people? Parliament ceded to our demand to repeal the Stamp Act because our boycott had cost them dearly. Already the women are spinning and a few landowners are increasing their livestock to supply them with wool and farmers are planting flax for cloth. We only need weavers to complete that entire line of manufactory. But we can do more. We will be asking the people to step up to do that in other areas as well. Read on!"

> And whereas it is the opinion of this Town, that
> divers new Manufactures may be set up in America,
> to its great Advantage, and some others carried to a
> greater Extent, particularly those of Glass & Paper[33]

"Already have somebody in Milton looking for rags to make paper, Eli. In fact, a cart went through here only last week picking up rags for just that purpose."

"And Otis is ready to move forward with this plan?"

"Of course! The entire idea of this new non-consumption boycott serves Boston by improving our economy while at the same time showing Britain that we're not going to be docile as lambs while they pillage our purses."

He paused while searching for yet another paper for me to read.

> "Here's our promise to the Massachusetts Bay Colony:"
> in Order to extricate us out of these embarrassed and
> distressed   Circumstances,   to   promote   Industry,

---

[33] *Boston-Gazette, and Country Journal,* November 2, 1767.

Oeconomy and Manufactures among ourselves, and by this Means prevent the unnecessary Importation of European Commodities, the excessive Use of which threatens the Country with Poverty and ruin – DO promise and engage, to and with each other, that we will encourage the Use and consumption of all Articles manufactured in any of the British American Colonies, and more especially in this Province:; and that we will not, from and after the 31st of *December* next ensuing, purchase any of the following Articles, imported from Abroad, viz., *Loaf Sugar,* and all the other articles enumerated above. [34]

---

[34] *Boston-Gazette, and Country Journal,* November 2, 1767.

Molly Weston

Business at the tavern was slowing down. Although we still had some of the dock workers drinking and eating, the numbers had dwindled. One-by-one, the dockhands stopped coming in. Many lacked the money to frequent our establishment. *We need another source of revenue. Something new to offer. Something to bring in customers.*

I was exasperated with the situation at the tavern. Revenue was one reason, another was that with mother so busy of late with her spinning classes, much of the food preparation and cooking for the tavern guests fell to me. I know that my biscuits weren't as tasty, and though the men didn't complain, every now and again I would see a lip curl slightly as I set the victuals in front of them.

Grabbing the *Gazette*, I took to perusing the advices. Longer letters and articles would keep till evening, but scanning the short advices always proved informative. At the bottom of the first page, however, an advice caught my eye. Visions of the warm drink spiced with cayenne and cardamom made my mouth water.

A Machine, the newest that has been made in *Boston*, to grind Chocolate, and will be warranted. Likewise, a Cleaner of Cocoa for chocolate, fit to grind 500wt. in Ten Hours. This Mill is warranted to grind 14wt. in Two Hours. Any Gentleman inclining to purchase the above Machine, may have it a Pennyworth for Cash. The same is to be Sold by *Henry Snow* in Temple-Street, New-Boston————Choice Chocolate made and Sold by said *Snow*.[35]

---

[35] *Boston-Gazette, and Country Journal*, November 30, 1767.

"Father, this machine could be the answer." I approached him as he sat by the hearth in the great room, pipe in hand and feet outstretched towards the glowing embers of the dying fire.

"Oh, Molly, have you any idea of the cost of such a machine? And besides, sailors aren't much into drinking chocolate."

"But he's selling it cheaply. Right here it says, 'a pennyworth for cash.' You are making my argument. Have you any idea how many sailors I served today? Five. Five! We used to serve 30 at a time. If we expand our drink offerings, we could turn The Three Lions into a coffee house, serve chocolate and scones during the day to women, and we could grind chocolate and sell it to the other coffee houses, and —"

"You'd turn my tavern into a coffee house for women?"

My idea was a sound one; I hadn't expected such an outburst.

"Have you not thought of why Henry Snow would be selling his machine? Perhaps his customers for chocolate have dwindled as much as our own for ale."

It was obvious that father wasn't as enamored of my plan to increase our income. I sighed, grabbed the paper, and retreated to the kitchen to roll out the dough for tomorrow's pasties. Perhaps father was right. If we weren't conducting much business, others were likely to experience the same downturn. Maybe Mr. Snow wasn't selling as much chocolate as I'd first thought.

✦

After another afternoon visiting shops and getting only a few more signatures for the nonimportation petition, I stopped into Anna's. Most of the women had packed up for the day, and I joined mother in storing all the yarn and thread that had been spun.

"Today was a good day, Molly," she said as I grabbed a few skeins of yarn.

"How much did you spin?"

139

"It wasn't as much as our sisters in Middleton," she replied. We had read that the Daughters of Liberty in that city had joined forces and woven over 20,000 yards of cloth.[36] Though I was good with numbers, I couldn't do the necessary figures in my head to determine how many skeins that would be.

"But then we are only eight and they are 180," she continued.

"Well, you might soon have an outlet for your work. Joshua Upham and a few other gentlemen are building a woolen manufactory with a spinning room. Can you imagine how much we can do with enough space to spin, weave and sew?"[37]

"Don't forget that several farming gentlemen soon will be raising sheep," Anna said. "Can you imagine the sight of one thousand sheep in the fields outside of Boston? Or sheep wandering among the cattle and British regulars on the Common?"[38]

"How wonderful it will be to have a dedicated space for our work!" Mother exclaimed. "Finally, our efforts will result in clothing made here in America."

"I do trust they will have a high standard of quality," said Anna. "It will be important that the women not feel as if they are wearing homespun, even if they are."

"Mother! Anna! That won't be the issue at all!" I insisted. "The reason you are spinning and why Mr. Upham is building a manufactory is so that Americans may become independent of

----

[36] The women in Middleton, MA had woven 20,522 yards of cloth in 1769. Nash, G. B. 2005. *The unknown American Revolution: The unruly Birth of Democracy and the struggle to create America.* New York: NY: Viking Penguin.

[37] *Boston-Gazette, and Country Journal,* October 28, 1768.

[38] *Boston-Gazette, and Country Journal,* October 28, 1768.

British imports. The Body of the People began this movement toward spinning, and as such, I believe that our ladies will be proud to wear American."

"I hope you are right. I must admit to being a little overwhelmed at all this." Mother turned and waved her arm at the shelves of yarn in various colors and different-sized skeins. "I haven't spun thread and yarn since I was a girl. Once Anna opened her shop, there was no reason to spend time on that chore."

Anna had been sweeping up mouse-sized balls of fluff that had gathered in the corners of the room. Each swish of the bristles set them a-flying, only to settle behind the broom. Truly it was a fruitless task she had undertaken.

I unfolded the *Gazette* I had been carrying in my apron pocket. "Listen to this:"

> Peter Etter & Sons are selling worsted stocking, thread and cotton, milled yard and worsted yard, cotton gloves, knit patterns for wastcoats and breeches, milled yarn caps for seamen (especially whalers and cod fishermen). As the above-mentioned Goods have been sufficiently try'd and the Goodness and Wear approv'd, they hope for Encoragement, and will be greatly oblig'd to any Gentleman for the Favour of this custom—Town or Country Traders that will bespeak any Quantity, on paying down the Money, shall have a Discount of 10 per Cent, or will advance for Three Months, in order to procure a greater Stock, a 12 pCt.[39]

---

[39] *Boston-Gazette, and Country Journal*, November 9, 1767.

"If Etter & Sons are looking to sell American made garments, and all the papers are talking about women wearing homespun, and everyone knows we are spinning and weaving our own cloth . . ." she began, but then stopped short. Mother and I turned to look at the shop owner.

After a short pause, the corners of her mouth turned up and then her teeth peeked through and her eyes began to twinkle.

"Let's have a contest!"

Mother and I exchanged glances, but I could see that she was immediately taken with the idea.

"Of course! We could get all the women in Boston to compete with Cambridge. Maybe we could even involve Middleton, though it's a bit further."

Anna continued, "And we could get someone to judge the quality and someone to tally the skeins . . ."

Mother jumped in. "Each town would need these judges. And we would need to announce the contest."

"But first to set the date."

I left the two women to make their plans, knowing that I would be the one to ensure all the newspapers helped us publicize the event. Perhaps mother and Anna are correct in their thinking, I mused. If we could make our spinning and weaving effort well known throughout the colonies, certainly all the women would see the value in purchasing our fabrics.

The Town Meeting had passed a resolution for women to forego imported dresses, and it went so far as to suggest that the city provide classes in spinning for all women and children. Peter Oliver, father-in-law to Governor Hutchinson's daughter, had been speaking ill of the practice to any who would listen. More than once I heard people say he believed the spinning classes were "another scheme" concocted by radicals "to keep up the ball of contention."[40] But by

November, all the papers were proposing that American women should wear homespun. The *Gazette*'s letter gave us even more desire to carry on with mother's plans for spinning.

> *To the* LADIES *of* NORTH AMERICA.
>
> Ladies,
>
> I AM one of those who think it not only high Time but of the last Importance, that you should be publickly addressed . . . I venture to lay at your Feet a few well-intended Sentiments, which tho' in d plain homspun Garb, I hope will not offend. I am convinced that at this present it is not only in your Inclination and Will, but also in your Power, to effect more in Favour of your Country, than an Army of a Hundred Thousand Men; and indeed more than all the armed Men on this vast Continent? . . . All I think at present that can be reasonably expected or desired of you, is to consent to lay aside all superfluous Ornaments for a Season—after which they shall be surely returned to you again with Interests. —You shall be cloathed in Purple, and Scarlet, and Fine Linnen of our own, and with other glorious Apparel; which, if possible, shall add a Lustre to your native Charms.

HENRY FLYNT[41]

---

[40] Nash, G. B. 2005. The unknown American Revolution: The unruly birth of democracy and the struggle to create America. New York: NY: Viking Penguin. p. 143.

[41] *Boston-Gazette, and Country Journal*, November 2, 1767, p. 2.

Reading Mr. Flynt's letter uplifted our spirits. It would take a lot of convincing to convince Mercy Otis Warren and her friends of the need to give up their fine Italian silks. But if Mercy were to buy and wear homespun, I was certain that our cause would succeed. With paper in hand, I set off for the Warren home, practicing my persuasive reasoning along the way.

Hester Winslow

"Hester! Hester!"

I paused when I heard my name, but couldn't imagine who would have such poor manners as to shout out my Christian name in such a way on the street. *What a shameless individual!*

My surprise was doubled, however, when I saw Cotton Easton running towards me, red-faced and out of breath.

"Whatever is the matter with you? Is that any way to address a lady?" I turned my back to leave the wretch to reconsider his upbringing.

"We need to talk."

"We? Whatever would we have to say to one another?"

"I may have some information you could use."

My spine stiffened at his tone as well as the words.

"Whatever do you mean?" I asked sweetly.

"Meet me at Copp's Hill, across from the North Water Mill tomorrow evening."

"Meet you at the cemetery? Are you daft? Why ever would I go there in the evening?"

The light breeze caught my words and carried them away in silence. I had to think quickly. Something was afoot and I needed to learn more.

"Fine. I'll see you there at 8. It should be dark enough by then to avoid being recognized by anyone."

"Till then." Cotton doffed his cap and bowed low, a faux knight being dismissed by his ladylove.

I was still annoyed by his actions when I arrived home, but now I needed to busy myself with a costume for the morrow. Cotton couldn't expect me to be seen in the northern most part of Boston at dusk, in the cemetery(!), looking like the lady I am. *Certainly, Cyrus has some older breeches and a coat that will suit me.*

Outfitted in Cyrus' worst, I headed toward the cemetery. As long as I kept my head down, nobody bothered to greet me. Most of the people I encountered were men, and I was not inclined to try to lower my voice to pass as a male. And although I had taken care to darken by cheeks and chin with ash, should anyone look too closely, they would see my stubble was smoothed on. My husband's smallest trousers were still too large, so I had tied them closed with a length of rope, which kept coming loose. That kept my hands in my coat pockets to hold up my trousers, which caused my traditional gait to sway side to side, more of a sailor's swagger than a lady's stroll.

I had nearly reached the end of Prince Street, any further and I would have ended up at Gee's Wharf, but then out of the shadows stepped my new confederate. He, too, had taken care to disguise his general appearance. A Monmouth cap covered his blonde tresses, and a hunting shirt, fringed at all the edges, covered his traditional checkered shirt.

"Be quick about it." I couldn't help but look side to side and over his shoulder in a continuous loop.

"Slow down, missy."

My eyes snapped back to his. Never had anyone addressed me with such impudence! But his tone was serious enough that I paid heed.

"You've been working Molly over pretty well. I'm not sure why you've got a bee in your head to make her life miserable . . .. No, let me finish.

"I've been thinking about that June celebration at the Common, and as I look back on it, you were quite pleased with my being overshadowed by Lt. Canfield. Now, a good friend might have found the scene a bit disconcerting and gone to the aid of her friend. You, however, stayed back and showed her no concern at all. My conclusion is that you are not a friend, but rather a foe. For what reason, I don't know, and I truly don't care."

He paused, as if to breathe, but the hesitation was for the words that came next.

"Yes, very well, let's get on with it. To put your bee at rest, you need to know more about Lt. Geoffrey Canfield. Let's walk a bit."

He took my arm and led me down Ferry Way, but soon enough I pulled my arm away.

"Wouldn't look good for you to be escorting me, dressed like this, that is."

I could barely make out a faint smile in the fading light, and then he told me the most fantastic story about Molly, Eli, and the Lt. Geoffrey Canfield.

November 1767

Geoffrey Canfield

My platoon was being kept busy as we served more and more Writs of Assistance. This morning, I found myself facing General Bridgewater as he huffed around his office. Once again, I was standing at attention watching through non-seeing eyes as General Bridgewater paced his ersatz office.

The man shuffled papers on the right, restacked papers on the left; he could never find anything on that cluttered desk. Still, I remained at attention, waiting for my superior to produce the writ in question. My ears fixed on the grandfather clock standing to the side of the desk, its pendulum's repetitive tick-tock ordering me to stay alert.

"Here! Take your men over to the harbor. Warehouse over there storing munitions."

His eyes looked up though his head was bent down, and they peered at me intently. I felt a shiver down my spine. The pendulum moved back and forth, ticking away the seconds. *Did he know about the mill?*

I stiffened my spine a bit further and found myself holding my breath. My right foot stepped forward so I could reach the writ, but the general wouldn't release it.

"Sir?" I stepped back into attention.

"Lieutenant, it's come to my attention that of all the writs your platoon has served, you have yet to seize any contraband."

My insides stiffened.

"Sir?"

"Don't play daft. You and your platoon have been serving writs for weeks. Not one has resulted in your confiscating smuggled goods. What do you say?"

I struggled to control my bodily functions, specifically the coloring I could feel rising in my face. The ticking clock grew louder. *Deep breaths. Breathe deeply. Don't lose control.*

"Sir, there was never an indication of smuggled goods. Nothing to confiscate."

That wasn't necessarily true, but surely, he didn't know that. To be honest, I had kept my men from searching, relying on Eli and his instantaneous mobs to threaten us with violence so that we could walk away on the pretense of keeping the peace. *What does he know?*

"Be advised, lieutenant, that I will be keeping a close watch on your duties. We must keep an eye on all munitions, whether they be smuggled or stored illegally. Especially with these lawless colonists, ready to riot at a moment's notice."

He finally raised his head and I felt his eyes running over me, searching for any facial tic or other indication of betrayal. My eyes were fixed on Copley's painting — I wouldn't let myself look at the general for fear of giving away the truth. If he didn't know what had happened to his cache of munitions, all he really did know was that my platoon hadn't seized any smuggled goods. That action would be easier to refute in a military court, should it ever come to a trial. Outright insubordination would have to be proved, and that would be difficult to do.

After what seemed like minutes, he walked around the desk and placed himself inches from my face.

"Don't disappoint."

The threat was clear. We had to come back with the smuggled goods. I looked down at the name on the writ. John Hancock.

Eli Weston

Another writ! The number of writs being issued was beyond all reason. Customs officers delighted in bringing forth charges against citizens of all sorts, from shopkeepers to merchants, to ship captains, and now to one of Boston's leading citizens. I hurried to gather my men, and Henry had run out to do the same as soon as he heard the news. I hoped we would arrive in time to halt the destruction Canfield believed would come to pass.

We arrived, unfortunately, after Canfield's platoon had already begun their search. The red coats were on a hunt, looking for anything that hinted at munitions — kegs filled with black powder, musket balls, even firearms. Soldiers pried open crates and hurled the wooden lids aside in their rush to find anything to indict Hancock. Not a single crate escaped their crowbars. Wooden lids cluttered the floor, and after inspecting the crates, heavy boots stomped the boards, splintering the wooden squares and circles into kindling.

My men halted momentarily to take in the scene, and when it revealed itself for the disaster it was, they rushed the lobster backs. They aggressively attacked the soldiers, beating them with cudgels. Fists flew and many a kick was landed before the soldiers gathered their wits about them to retaliate. Fortunately for us, the soldiers had laid aside their own weapons in order to open the crates. Yet unfortunately for us, they were now armed with hardened iron bars, which landed heavier blows than our wooden batons.

I couldn't say how long the brawling lasted, but once it ended, everyone had been bloodied. A few noses were broken on both sides, perhaps some ribs as well. Eyes were blackening and swelling shut, and moans were heard more than any other sound.

"Pick up, men. We're heading out."

Canfield's voice pierced the complaints of the wounded, and when I looked up at him, I could see that he, too, had suffered in the

150

fisticuffs. His left cheek was cut and still oozed red, although I could see that earlier the blood had flowed freely down his white lapels. Scraped knuckles ended in swollen fingers that clenched his firearm in a vice-like grip. The soldiers groaned and shuffled their way through the warehouse, kicking aside the broken crates and anyone lying in their path.

Geoffrey Canfield

"Well, I see that you, too, took part in last night's scuffle. What did you find?"

General Bridgewater had wasted no time in calling me to his office the day after the Hancock raid.

"Nothing, sir."

"Didn't I tell you that smuggled munitions were housed there? Are you and your men so blind and inept that you can't see what's in front of you?"

"Sir, if I could explain."

"No, you cannot! I sent you to Hancock's warehouse with the express purpose of bringing back what he has smuggled. How dare you return empty-handed!"

I opened my mouth once again, but was silenced immediately by my commander's scowling face. *Better to remain quiet for the time being.*

The general paced behind his desk. From time to time, he would mutter words I couldn't quite hear, then fall silent for a few more paces before mumbling something else.

"At least you have something to show for your futile efforts."

"Sir?"

"This time, at least, you showed that you're working for the Crown and not the rabble in this wilderness they call a city."

♥

In my room that night, I polished my boots and burnished my buttons. Elizabeth had taken it upon herself to scrub my uniform coat and trousers, saying that only women knew how to get stains out of white wool. For me, I was happy to turn that duty over to someone else. My hands ached whenever I moved them, each knuckle knotted, swollen, and difficult to flex. Even the larger movement of back and forth of polishing caused discomfort and cramps.

"You know, Buttermilk," I said to the creamy yellow tabby, "the last two days haven't been good ones."

Every night, Molly's pet would greet me as I entered the kitchen, and then, much like a sheep dog, herd me up the stairs to the room we shared. I reached down to scratch her behind the ears. Loud purring filled the small second-story room, and when I leaned back into the chair to pick up my polishing cloth, the large cat leapt into my lap.

"Whoa!" I grabbed her by the sides and was about to set her on the floor, when I hesitated. She took advantage of that brief pause to squirm out of my grasp, lie down on my lap, and stretch out on her side. She was so large that once she was prone, she was as long as my thighs. Buttermilk turned her head upside down, exposing her neck. How could I not scratch her chin, rub her ears between my fingers, or gently run my hand the length of her flank? She continued to purr, and as I stroked the soft fur, I could feel my anxiety ease.

"Apparently this is what makes you so special," I whispered to the flirting feline. "You're definitely much more than a mouser."

Molly Weston

Mercy Warren agreed. When I laid out the idea of wearing homespun garments and showed her Mr. Flynt's published letter, she eagerly grasped the idea and made it her own.

"We'll talk to all the women of the upper sort immediately," she began. "Have you read the *Post-Boy* yet? This week's edition included this 'Address to the Ladies,'" she said and began to read aloud:

> Young ladies in town, and those that live round,
> Let a friend at this season advise you:
> Since money's so scarce, and times growing worse
> Strange things may soon hap and surprize you:
> First then, throw aside your high top knots of pride
> Wear none but your own country linnen;
> Of Oeconomy boast, let your pride be the most
> To show cloaths of your own make and spinning.
> What, if homespun they say is not quite so gay
> As brocades, yet be not in a passion,
> For when once it is known this is much wore in town,
> One and all will cry out, 'tis the fashion!
> And as one, all agree that you'll not be married be
> To such as will wear London Fact'ry:
> But at first sight refuse, tell 'em such you do chuse
> As encourage our own Manufact'ry.
> No more Ribbons wear, nor in rich dress appear,
> Love your country much better than fine things,
> Begin without passion, 'twill soon be the fashion
> To grace your smooth locks with a twine string.[42]

The Boston Post-Boy & Advertiser wasn't a paper I read regularly, although upon hearing of the publisher's slant, I wanted to run out and purchase a copy.

"Surely wearing the ribbons we already have would be suitable, don't you think? I cannot imagine tying my hair up with twine. What a vision I would make!" Mercy laughed. "But I do believe that we are being called upon to do our part. As for me, I intend to dress down."

She looked at me with a gleam in her eye. "It seems that our women will be wearing brown this year after all!"

---

[42] *Boston Post-Boy & Advertiser,* November 16, 1767.

Eli Weston

Cotton and Paul are after me to join them in the forests. The pay is good, and with the embargo in full force, dockworkers are spending more time in taverns than earning their livelihood. Still, I am unsure about leaving the wharf where I have worked since I was 16. There is a comfort in having mastered the work and earned the respect of my fellow dockworkers. Ship captains know me as well, and that has given me great freedom to work on behalf of the Sons of Liberty. The captains, and the merchants they sail for, have trusted me to see that contraband goods are spirited away in the darkest of night.

On the other hand, a cold wind is blowing from across the Atlantic and Writs of Assistance have become more commonplace. As such, the customs officers administer their own justice. They are aided by merchants loyal to Parliament, as well as Hutchison and Bernard. And they are quiet about who they turn in. Should I continue working at the wharf these days, I could jeopardize any efforts of the Sons of Liberty.

"There's more work in logging than at Long Wharf anyway," Paul said. "You can do much better felling white pine than unloading cargo that can't be sold."

He shoved a torn piece of newspaper into my hand. I couldn't believe what I was seeing.

> TO BE SOLD
> About 30 Thousand of choice
> White Oak Plank, 2, $2^{1/2}$ and 3
> Inch—Also a Parcel of White
> Oak Barrel Staves.
> Inquire of Edes & Gill[43]

"Is this what you're doing?"

"We provide timber for His Majesty's Royal Navy, brother, and if an occasional log isn't accounted for, who's to say it's missing?"

My brother was turning into a rogue and I loved him for his bravery.

Paul and Cotton had returned to Boston to replenish their supply of foodstuffs for the logging camp. Cotton was dawdling in the kitchen, still looking for a chance to speak with Molly, but for me, today would be an excuse to spend some time drinking and catching up with my younger brother.

"You've seen the news about Spain and the warships they're building. And you've the seen advices for purchasing timber. Every week, Edes is publishing one or the other. His Majesty is in the ship-building business these days."

"Here, look at this," Paul shoved an advice across the table and pointed to the third column.

HALIFAX, Careening-Yard, *October* 1, 1767
WHEREAS, there will be Wanted by the 10th of *March* next, for His Majesty's Service here, 134 Ton of streight square Oak Timber:

        Inches.   Inches.

    12 by 12 not less than 23 Feet long and as (much longer as can be got.

49 Ton 12 by 16   16 Feet
29 Ton fr. 8 to 11 Square fr. 9 to 13 Feet
15 Ton 12 by 12   17 Feet

---

[43] *Boston-Gazette, and Country Journal,* October 5, 1767.

6 Ton 12 to 16	16 to 20 Feet
20 Ton 12 to 16	28 to 30 Feet
10 Ton Ditto	14 & 15 Feet

263 Tons

69 Ton of Square Pine Timber 15 by 12 Inches, 23 Feet long. 3200 Feet of Pine Joist, running Measure, 9 by 3 Inches, 10, 20, or 30 Feet long. 65000 Feet of Pine Boards and Plank.
16000 Feet Oak Plank of 8 Inches from
(20 t0 23 Feet long and upwards.
4750 Ditto, Ditto, 4-Inches ditto, Plank Measure.
492 Thousand of Shingles, clear of Sap
27 Thousand Clap Boards, Ditto
150 Spars of 5 6 and 7 Inches.
120 Hogsheads of Stone Lime.
166 Barrels of Tar.
8 Barrels of Train Oyl.

WHOEVER has a Mind to contract for supplying the above Materials, either the Whole or in Part, to be landed at his Majesty's Yard here, by the Time aforesaid, are desired to send in their Proposals sealed, to the Store-keeper, at his Office in said Yard, on or before the 20th of November next, that a Contract or Contracts may be made with the Person or Persons who make Proposal most advantageous for the Government.
Joseph Gerrish, Store keeper and Naval-Officer.[44]

Paul quaffed his beer and wiped his sleeve across his mouth. "And we're in the timber-supplying business." What remained unsaid was the amount of timber that we would hold back from the Crown's surveyor.

"It's a deal." I clinked my pewter tankard against his and we raised a glass to our new venture.

✦

Loading and unloading cargo on Long Wharf was backbreaking work, but it hadn't prepared me at all for felling trees. I had always considered myself to be a fit man, but it seemed I had grown new muscles overnight once I started working in the forests. Muscles I had long forgotten I had now reminded me of their existence. Paul shared some liniment with me to ease the discomfort, but it served another purpose as well. It helped to keep the bugs at bay. I hadn't been prepared for the multitude of flying, biting insects. Clouds of the tiny black creatures would wrap themselves around my head like a towel. To counteract the onslaught of bugs, we used folded kerchiefs to swaddle our noses and mouths to keep them out while we breathed. Paul had a liniment for their bites too. We eagerly awaited the colder weather to send those critters to their grave.

The white pine grew to heights of 80 to 100 feet, and these tallest were the ones that had been marked for the King. Once in Portsmouth or Newcastle, they would become the masts of the newest men-of-war. When I worked on the dock, most of the loading was straightforward, simply stack the bales or crates high and tight. Much more precision was required in logging. Trees had to be

---

[44] *Boston-Gazette, and Country Journal*, November 2, 1767.

chopped and sawed in a certain way, at fairly precise angles, so they would fall in a particular direction. Preferably away from other loggers. Once down, the branches would be sawn off till only the trunk remained. Then we wrapped the trunk in chains, and teams of horses, or sometimes oxen, would haul the giant mass away. Some of the younger boys on the crew would chop the branches into logs suitable for fuel and once they had a cord, they would haul it into town to sell.

Although Paul had convinced me to come to the forest, it was Cotton who showed me the ropes.

"We're looking only for the trees with three hatchet marks, the King's broad arrow. You'll find it on trees that are two feet in diameter near the ground." Cotton walked over to a good-sized tree and pointed with his axe to the broad arrow sign.

"Then, you'll need to determine how it'll fall."

He laughed when he saw the quizzical look on my face.

"Easily done, my friend. Look up and see which way the tree leans. You'll want to make your notch on the leaning side. Here." He slapped the tree to make his point.

Once Cotton had explained the process, he and I felled a tree, and then I was left on my own. After a couple of days, I was as good as he, and as was our custom, we began to wager. Some days on who could fell the most trees, or the tallest, or the largest in diameter. Some days we would select like-sized trees and race to fell and strip them. It wasn't long before I could best his times.

Molly Weston

I sighed and glanced at a small advice in the upper corner of the *Gazette* that Father had left on the table and was surprised to see that the periodical was still publishing the advice of Lt. Governor Hutchinson's book for sale. Benjamin must be getting paid a nice sum for each instance of printing it:

Just Published,
And to be had in *Union-Street*, opposite to
the Cornfield,
The HISTORY of the Province of
MASSACHUSETS-BAY,
From the Charter of K. William & Q. Mary
in 1691, until the year 1750.
By Mr. HUTCHINSON,
Lieutenant Governor of the Province
To be had at the same Place,
The History of the MASSACHUSETS
from its original Settlement to the Year 1692.
By the same Author.[45]

Ha! As if anyone would buy anything from this liar. It would be interesting, however, to read his opinions of what had been happening since he had thrown his support behind Andrew Oliver, the so-called Stamp Master. But then, all of Boston knew Hutchinson was Parliament's lackey in the Massachusetts Bay Colony, so perhaps there wouldn't be much of interest after all. I would have given anything to talk to Eli about this book. The brother who taught me

---

[45] *Boston Evening-Post*, August 3, 1767.

to read would certainly have an opinion to share. But with both Eli and Paul in the forest, that conversation would have to wait.

I felt the loss of companionship with my brothers gone. Life was quieter without two of them. It wasn't only that I missed working with them every day; it was sensing their absence that upset me. Where Eli should have been sitting at the hearth, only our dog Boots remained curled in a tight spiral. Where Paul should have been pouring ale and rum behind the bar, either Father or Henry filled in.

The Three Lions felt empty, even with a full house of redcoats and sailors. Raucous laughter should have chased away the hollowness within my soul. Instead, the noise grated like two cats screeching at one another in the alley at night. Everything felt wrong. And a bit more dangerous.

More rooms upstairs now were filled with additional soldiers we quartered, space that rightfully belonged to my family. Some of the soldiers had begun to insult us, for being tavern owners, and they were disrespectful of our gender. Mother and I were used to rude behavior displayed by drunken sots, but there was an edgy tone to the soldiers' bearing that was distressing. They, too, felt the absence of our protectors and feared no reprisal for insolent behavior. So far, they hadn't acted on any beastly intentions, but I felt certain that moment would come.

I shivered thinking about some of the leers we endured and mopped the table more vigorously, as if I could vanquish those thoughts. Others quickly surfaced to replace them. I looked over at Father and it was hard not to feel bitter about having to feed and shelter redcoats when our tavern could have been taking in money from real, paying guests. New York refused to house the soldiers, but Parliament quickly punished them for disobedience. Still, I wished that Boston had the courage to defy the Quartering Act like their Colony's legislative House did, even if Parliament would punish us just the same.

My musings were interrupted by stomping feet and a slamming door.

"Molly, come quick!"

I hurried into the kitchen toward Geoffrey's voice. He was drinking thirstily by the time I had rounded the corner.

"Your brothers Eli and Paul. They've been arrested." He was still out of breath and his words were clipped and harsh.

"No!" My knees buckled and I collapsed to the floor while burying my head in my hands.

"Come, come." Geoffrey gently coaxed me onto a bench and sat with his arm around my shoulders."

"We *will* get them back."

"Oh, how can you say that? I don't know how that could ever happen. Once they are in jail, only a trial will free them. Oh, my goodness! A trial! How can we hope for a fair hearing? And a lawyer? How can we pay for a lawyer? Who will defend them?" My head was spinning with all the consequences of their imprisonment while a separate part of my mind rummaged through the names of friends and acquaintances who would or could help. But then another thought, one more concerning, burst through.

"What about Cotton?"

Geoffrey stiffened at the mention of my brother's friend, and though he tried to hide it, a bit of hostility colored his response.

"Cotton escaped the raid; he's fine. Eli and Paul hied south when they heard of the raid and fell directly into the hands of my platoon. Cotton, well, obviously he ran another direction. We didn't encounter him anywhere."

"You mean you arrested them? How could you?" I pulled away from his embrace not wanting to believe what I was hearing.

"Molly, I didn't have a choice. My men came upon a group of the loggers and captured Eli and Paul before I had a chance to intervene. It all happened so suddenly."

His tone took on a softer tone. "I would have wished a different ending than what transpired."

My stomach churned with this news. I wrapped my arms around me and bent at the waist, hoping to squeeze out the turmoil that had taken root in my belly. Geoffrey tried to console me, softly stroking my back while I tried to breathe.

"Cotton will turn up, right? And he won't be arrested now that he's not in the forest?"

"Our hands are busy with those that we've captured. Mine doubly so as I'll need to assess your brothers' situation and come up with an escape plan."

I sat up quickly and sucked in my breath.

He looked directly into my eyes. "I *will* get them out."

✦

If then Americans are free British subjects, and cannot be represented in parliament, it is plain they cannot be taxed by the British parliament, consistent with the British constitution: further, if the design of erecting the power of legislation here was to preserve this right of representation to the subjects in America, does not the taxing them in Britain where they are not represented defeat that design, and render the power in this instance a nullity? No one at this time will say that the people of America are not taxed by the parliament: The act is already in force: Every man that shall make use of Glass, Painter's Colours or Paper, hereafter to be imported, will feel it: So will every *woman* that drinks her dish of tea: at least they will *pay* for it if they do not *feel* it. I wish then that the True Patriot, Amicus, or any writer on that side, would prove if they can, that the exercise of parliamentary jurisdiction in levying taxes on the colonists, either external or internal, while they are not and cannot be represented, does not effectually overthrow the legislative power in America; or that it can be consistent with any degree of freedom. . ..[46]

Sam Adams is at it again. Taxation without Representation! That was his rallying cry two years ago, and now he has resurrected it.

I stowed the paper near father's chair. He'll be wanting to read it once the evening crowd thinned. Surely, he and Sam will be talking about it this evening. With Eli and Paul in prison, Sam's made an effort to come into The Three Lions to visit with Father. The two huddle together and their voices drop to a whisper whenever anyone comes near. Father has tried to pick up with the Sons of Liberty since Eli's imprisonment, but with two workers gone, he is barely able to keep the tavern running, even with Henry's help. But goodness! They even look suspicious just sitting there!

I couldn't worry about one more thing. With Eli and Paul in prison and Hester on the rampage, I had more on my hands than I could manage. Father was on his own.

Grabbing my woolen cloak, I headed for the door.

---

[46] *Boston-Gazette, and Country Journal*, November 23, 1767.

December 1767

Geoffrey Canfield

Making that promise to Molly was proving easier than keeping it. Eli, Paul, and four other loggers had been imprisoned in Needham, about 20 miles from Boston, the closest settlement to the forested area where they'd been apprehended. Our jailer was a tavern keeper, loyal to the Crown, who offered up a room in which to hold the loggers, for a fee, of course. General Bridgewater was inordinately delighted upon hearing we had captured a group of illegal loggers, and consequently, he signed the owner's expense voucher with a flourish of his quill.

Molly was having more luck than I at finding persons to assist her brothers and the other loggers. The labyrinthine quest she undertook began with one of her shop clientele, Mercy Warren, sister to James Otis, a locally known solicitor. Mrs. Warren, as I understand, then approached her brother about the situation. Molly's father also pursued some help in the cause with solicitors Samuel Adams and John Adams.

While the American lawyers worked on building a case against the Crown, I surveyed the situation from the British angle. Had Eli and Paul not been taken into custody by my men, I would have had more flexibility in how they were treated. As it was, too many regulars had been in on their capture. One man's word against so many didn't amount to much, even if it was the word of their superior. No, I needed a more drastic measure to employ on their behalf. What that measure was, however, I still had no idea.

And in the back of my mind, I could still hear her asking about Cotton. I thought we had reconciled that issue, and my reasoning told me it was so. My heart, however, was ill at ease thinking she might still harbor feelings for her first infatuation. I needed to close the door on that uneasiness as it would only breed more suspicion.

Molly Weston

Hester is needling me again. With Eli and Paul in jail, I try to spend more time at the shop to forget our troubles. Today, I was working on a display of some newly arrived fans. They were beautifully made; peacock feathers cut so intricately and woven together so that once a fan was open, glistening blues and greens formed a full tail of the colorful fowl. The delicacy of the fan contrasted sharply with the harpy who tailed me like a duckling its mother, chattering about how fortunate she was to have left the single life behind by becoming a *feme covert*. Her favorite topic of discussion these last weeks was the importance of being married. Or to be more accurate, her insistence that being a married woman was preferable to being single.

"Cyrus is such a good provider. Did you know that we hired a cook?"

Hester was circling the display table, her delicate fingers dancing lightly across the array of winter gloves.

"I see you've been wearing some new gloves," she began.

"Yes, they were a gift." *Oh! I should not have said that!*

"A gift?"

I couldn't tell her the truth. A lie would have to do. *Forgive me, Reverend Howard!*

"From my brother Eli. He knew that my older pair were beyond mending."

"Hmm." Her tone let me know she didn't believe me. For a brief moment, I hoped we could move on from the verbal sparring, but I was mistaken.

"You cannot imagine how wonderful it is to not have to worry about meal preparation. All that measuring and stirring . . . it's so tedious!"

I needed to put a stopper in that mouth. The incessant chattering was grating and her last comment cut me deeply. Who wouldn't like to have someone else to do the cooking and baking and washing and marketing . . . the list of chores was endless for those who didn't have money, for someone like me.

She fingered some Irish lace and peeked through the tatted fabric.

I turned away lest I lose my temper at her cruel comments.

Covered? Protected? Well, she'll be in a pretty spot if Cyrus dies and leaves her penniless.
Scarcely had that thought crossed my mind when something worse tumbled out of my mouth.

"There's no shame in being a *feme sole*," I countered. "At least I will control my finances and future. The money I will earn, I will keep. You, on the other hand, could find yourself taking in boarders if you don't have any children soon. Without Cyrus paying the bills, you might actually have to cook!"

Hester gasped, astonished that I had found a backbone and, perhaps even more, dared to respond.

Once I started, I couldn't stop, and more rancor flew her way. "After all, you've been married nearly two years with nothing to show but your barrenness."

My mother would have said that last comment was unnecessarily spiteful, but I felt justified after enduring so much harsh criticism. And as soon as those sentiments were spoken, a palpable silence hung heavy between us.

Hester laid the delicate lace on the table and fussed with the edges so it lay flat.

Should I speak to her? Apologize? The months of her judging me with looks and words had taken a toll on my being. In the back of my mind, I could hear the Reverend Howard urging me to repent and apologize, but I couldn't bring myself to do it.

169

She looked up from the table, and waited a moment. Perhaps she was expecting that apology; however, my lips remained fixedly closed.

With a bang, the shop door flew open and in blew Mercy Warren.

"What a lovely day!"

I turned to greet my friend, and never had I been so happy to see her. But I was still so angry with Hester that I barely noticed when she narrowed her eyes and silently stepped out.

Hester Winslow

The nerve of that shop girl! And a tavern keeper's daughter to boot! How dare she talk to me like that! I couldn't believe my ears. Had Mercy Warren not entered at that moment, Molly would have been groveling for forgiveness.

That exchange occurred more than a week ago, but I still burned whenever I thought back on the day. One good result, however, was that it goaded me into disclosing my findings about Lt. Canfield with General Bridgewater.

I had been waiting for him once again in the coffee house, but when I simply couldn't bear the thought of another drink, I gathered up my belongings and rose to leave. Then, in strode the corpulent officer, his arms flinging front to back as he shook snow from his red woolen coat.

"There you are!" His voice reverberated throughout the establishment and one of the flinging arms pointed at me. The general's bluster had long since lost its power to command attention in this establishment, and the customers barely bothered to look up from their own private conversations to pay him heed.

A momentary lapse in judgment was giving me pique. Was it necessary to continue with my plan? But Molly's cutting remarks bubbled up and I resolved to follow through. I lifted my face to the raucous red whale swimming my way and smiled a welcome.

"Ah, my dear! There you are. This weather is dreadful. Cold to my bones, I am."

"Please join me, General Bridgewater. How wonderful to run into you again!"

"Perhaps a coffee to warm you, sir?" asked the attending boy.

Bridgewater looked the young lad up and down and then leaned in to peer into his eyes.

"Do I look as if I drink coffee, boy? Bring me tea, and a cup for the lady as well."

I had to smile. The coffee house we had been frequenting was owned by a loyalist, but the servants always erred on the side of caution by offering coffee first. Only a few knew of the owner's abundance of England's favorite beverage. William Shaw had been stockpiling crates of tea along with several other merchants who refused to sign the nonimportation agreement. A few other merchants had signed the letter but then quietly continued to sell tea to privileged customers, such as the general and Americans who steadfastly maintained their allegiance and fealty to the Crown. Those of us who were acquainted with one another knew where we would be served without having to risk exposure to and ridicule from the so-called patriots.

Once the tea was poured and the general had warmed his body as well as his mind to our conversation, it was my turn to lean in slightly.

"I understand that you have a Lt. Canfield under your command," I began.

Molly Weston

Henry has been attending the Sons of Liberty meetings. The youngest of my three brothers has stepped into the void left by the older two. Not only is he waiting on customers continually at The Three Lions, but he is working his way into the confidences of Paul Revere and Sam Adams. Last night, he was breathless when he returned from the Green Dragon. He tiptoed up to my room, and after a gentle knock, entered and swiftly closed the door. Putting his finger to his lips as if to silence me, he crossed the floor and simultaneously bent down to pat Boots on the head and sit at the foot of my bed.

"Any word on Eli and Paul?"

"No, Geoffrey says there isn't much he can do for a while. I'm hoping that they won't be sent to England for trial. You know there has been talk of doing such things."

"Sister, don't worry about that. You can trust in Geoffrey. He's been a solid ally these two years."

I felt my eyes well up and a tear from each dropped onto my cheeks. "I know." I sniffed and wiped my eyes. "What news have you?"

"James Otis has word from Pennsylvania. A lawyer, John Dickinson, recently wrote to advise him of some letters he'll be publishing in the *Pennsylvania Gazette*."

"Why should that concern us in Boston?"

"Dickinson will be publishing his letters anonymously, but his intent is to stir up the issue of taxation once again. He believes that the Townshend Act has the power to put America in peril."

"How so? How is it different from the Stamp Act? We beat back that Act of Parliament quite handily as I recall. And more merchants and shopkeepers have signed the nonimportation agreement. The boycott will work again, I'm sure."

"That's not the only thing, Molly. Dickinson says that our liberties are in imminent danger. The other colonies consider Boston, the whole Massachusetts Bay Colony actually, as the leader of the opposition, and we must be the ones to lead the charge against the Townshend Act."

"What is it that he expects us to do? Isn't the boycott enough? Certainly not more riots?" I shivered recalling the gangs of men and boys crashing through the streets, pillaging the offices of those who supported Great Britain's policy on taxes. Eli had been at the front of the first riot that ruined Andrew Oliver's stamp office. And so much damage had been done to other buildings and homes — windows smashed, houses broken into, gardens trampled — that there was still talk of bringing charges against the rioters and enforcing restitution payments.

"He didn't say, or at least Otis didn't talk about that. I guess we'll wait and see what develops."

The following day, as I dropped off the latest advice for Anna's shop, Benjamin Edes took me aside to show me the letter he had received from Mr. Dickinson. He quietly set type for the paper as I perused the pages that dealt with the issue of New York's opposition to quartering troops. He spoke of the quartering as an unjust tax on the colony and the injustice of Parliament's subsequent punishment.

IF the British Parliament has a legal authority to issue an order that we shall furnish a single article for the troops here, and to compel obedience to that order, they have the same right to issue an order for us supply those troops with arms, clothes, and every necessary, and to compel obedience to that order also; in short, to lay any burdens they please upon us. What is this but taxing us at a certain sum and leaving us only the manner of raising it?

As I continued to read, I saw that Henry had reached the correct conclusion — Parliament had placed America's liberties in a vulnerable position.

If the Parliament may lawfully deprive New York of any of her rights, it may deprive any or all the other colonies of their rights; and nothing can possibly so much encourage such attempts as a mutual inattention to the interests of each other. To divide, and thus to destroy, is the first political maxim in attacking those who are powerful by their union. [47]

"First Sam Adams stirs up his cry of Taxation without Representation again. And now this Pennsylvania farmer has all but issued a call to arms," I said to Benjamin, but mostly to myself. "And God help us all."

---

[47] *Pennsylvania Gazette,* December 3, 1767.

January 1768

Molly Weston

Henry is gone. We've spent hours looking for him, but no one claims to have seen him. Even Geoffrey and the other regulars who quarter at The Three Lions have spent time searching for my brother. Mother and Father are beside themselves, especially Mother. She always favored Henry above the other boys, and though he wasn't one to try her favoritism, he wasn't above testing it from time to time. Now, however, it had become obvious to everyone that Henry had befallen a calamitous event. Or perhaps worse someone with nefarious intent had maltreated our beloved Henry.

Father was the first to notice his absence.

"Where is that boy? He was supposed to be working by now."

Mother and I were chopping root vegetables for gobbet stew when he poked his head through the doorway.

"He said he had an errand and would be back soon," I replied, my eyes still on the rhythmic cuts I was making to the turnips. "Said something about the lottery."

"Ah! That blasted lottery is all he thinks about. It's become an infection in his brain!"

"That child does try your father's patience. The lottery winners haven't been announced yet. Do you think he went over to the *Gazette* to wheedle the names out of Benjamin?"

"Oh, it's doubtful that Ben would have the names, Mother, if they haven't held the drawing. Last we heard, they put off the drawing till late in January. Henry has to wait a couple more weeks before he can collect his prize!"

"That boy and his prize! Your father's right — it has become a brain disease with him."

But as the day wore on and Henry didn't return, everyone became agitated. With Eli and Paul in jail and Cotton in hiding, I felt the need to confide in Geoffrey when he returned from patrol that evening.

"It's so unlike him, Geoffrey. Henry has his faults, to be sure, but one of them is not leaving home without notice!"

I paced in front of the kitchen hearth as Geoffrey ate his supper. The second serving of the gobbet stew we had prepared earlier in the day was disappearing as I expanded my path to kitchen's four walls and rambled on about my brother.

My mind was so fixed on the situation that I hadn't realized Geoffrey had stood up until I ran into him.

"What? Oh." I tried to apologize, but he gripped my upper arms and forced me to look at him.

"Molly, stop. My men and I will go and search."

"But you, they, can't! It's Henry. Who knows where you will find him and what he might be involved in?"

"It's more important that we find the rascal than whatever he is doing. You and I know that until now he has barely been a part of the Sons of Liberty, and even now, he's more of an errand boy. It's unlikely that he would have been involved in anything serious and even more unlikely that any of my soldiers would even suspect him of being part of that group."

"But what if he is? If he's caught, like Eli and Paul," I couldn't bring myself to complete the thought.

"Don't even think like that! Ease your mind. Send your father to Revere's house to determine whether Henry is involved in anything. Then my men and I can freely search the city."

It was both a relief and a fright to learn from father that Henry's assistance hadn't been requested by Revere or other Sons of Liberty. All the same, I fretted that in some way he had become involved in an activity for which he could be punished and Geoffrey would be unable to help him.

Geoffrey Canfield

Molly's concern for her brother wasn't new, but the frantic nature of her request was. When Jonathan returned to say that none of the Sons of Liberty had required Henry's services that day, I mustered my three regulars to begin our hunt for the youngest Weston son.

Henry was well-known to us as we had all lived under the same roof for nearly a year and a half. The lad was coming into his own as a man, but still exhibited an ingenuous and guileless disposition from time to time. Of course, because of my close relationship with Eli, and now again with Molly, Henry had learned to be circumspect in his behaviors and speech around the regulars regarding our more immoderate deeds.

My men knew Henry to be quick to serve customers and attentive to replenishing food and drink. They didn't necessarily recognize that this swift service in the tavern extended to his legs. The boy could run like the wind, and it was this talent that, had he come across some trouble, I hoped had served him well.

We left The Three Lions and set out two-by-two in opposite directions. Knowing Henry's proclivities toward the Lottery, I sent two men toward the publishing house of Edes and Gill via Faneuil Hall, whose proprietors were operating the game of chance. Tension had been growing among those who had purchased tickets; the Lottery was to have been drawn in October, but the date had been pushed off several times and now wouldn't occur until later this month. I hoped that Henry had gone off to inquire as to the new date and then lost track of time while conversing with someone of interest or perchance decided to help a soul in need.

While they headed southwest, my man and I headed northeast toward the harbor to see whether the boy's interest in maritime activities might have led him in this direction. My heart's desire was that he had simply lost track of time in the city; should he have spent his day at the wharves, the Royal Navy midshipmen might have had a hand in the boy's disappearance.

We started at Clark's shipyard, the northernmost wharf in the city, then worked our way south to Hutchinson's Wharf and then Hancock's Wharf. We went door-to-door making inquiries of every merchant and warehouse manager. No one had seen Henry. Eventually, our quest was rewarded when we began to talk to seamen strolling through the darkened streets.

One particularly groggy fellow was leaning against some stacked bales when we approached. He was happy to have found someone who would listen to his ramblings.

"A fellow named Henry? Nah, never heard of him."

"A young lad, brownish hair, about this tall," I raised my hand to my nose.

"What's he done?"

I sighed out of exasperation. Although loquacious, this fellow may have tippled too much to be of use.

"Nothing. He's done nothing. We are looking for him." I spoke slowly so I wouldn't have to repeat myself.

"Well, then. Hmmph." The fellow looked to be thinking. "About this tall, you say? Could be, maybe, maybe not," he mumbled.

"Hurry up, mate." My subordinate stomped his feet in the cold. He was anxious to return to the tavern's warmth with a mug of ale at the ready.

I agreed that the sailor's tendency to tarry was exasperating, but I was determined to wait as long as necessary to pull out every detail he might know about Henry's whereabouts.

"Yes, I think it was him."

"You saw him? Where was he? What was he doing? Where did he go?"

The drunk peered up at me and paused. He sensed the urgency in my voice, but was slow and cautious in his reply, as if he were judging how much he could say freely.

"Those sailors took him they did. Round about midday it was. Yes, about then."

"Which ship?" I looked around to see whether any of the British ships were bustling with pre-sailing activity.

"Oh, she's long since gone. The *Hornet* Sloop of War, she was, from that mooring over there. Sailed at high tide."

I looked over my shoulder to the empty mooring the sailor was pointing at. My heart sank as I considered the implications of Henry being aboard such a ship. Captain Jeremiah Morgan was a blackguard of a seaman, and his crew sheltered more devils than Hell.

Oh, Henry! What have you gotten yourself into?

Eli Weston

We've been sitting in jail for several months now. Molly and Mother visit on a regular basis to provide us with food and drink. Without them, I fear we would have a more difficult time. When the weather turned, they provided blankets. Not only for me and Paul, but for the other loggers who were caught in Geoffrey's raid.

The jail is a frightful place. Before now, I had never given the plight of prisoners much thought. When we were first arrested, we found ourselves in a back room of a Royalist tavern in Needham. It wasn't large, but it felt more like home than this cell. After a couple of weeks, we were shackled and herded into a small wagon, with a web of poles for sides, where we struggled to get a comfortable sitting position. A sheriff drove the horse and cart while two British regulars escorted us on horseback to Watertown's jailhouse. The ride was long and cold. Every bump in the road traveled up through the wheels into the wagon bed and up through our spines. The jostling threw us against one other as well as the hard, wooden sides, but our driver never slowed. The frigid temperature ensured that our noses, ears, and fingers turned red and throbbed with pain, no matter how much we blew into our hands and covered our ears with our kerchiefs.

By the time we reached our new boarding house, our bodies were so cold and stiff we could barely crawl out of the wagon. Quickly they moved us into the new quarters we would share with four-legged roommates of varying sizes. The dank atmosphere the sheriff and town elders created when they built this place was as morbid as any English dungeon. Tiny windows high on the wall provided the only light. With winter's short days upon us, that left few hours with which to pass the time in activities other than conversation. Cloudy and stormy days left us with even fewer hours of sunlight.

The small windows also impeded the circulation of fresh air. The resultant stench, a combination of sweat and body odor along with the pungency of the relief bucket was heavy and foul when the regulars threw us in. Nowadays, that stench is barely perceptible to us so inured our noses have become to the constancy of the smell.

"Get up, Weston!" A sentry shouted at me as he neared the door. "You've got visitors."

The sentry had moved me to a more commodious cell where I could speak without other prisoners present. That action, too, must have been prearranged. My fingers quickly adjusted my clothing and combed through my hair, trying to make myself presentable for my callers. To my surprise, the next person I saw was my brother Paul.

"Eli!"

We embraced one another but didn't have much time to communicate before a deeper timbre of a male voice echoed in the corridor. I had expected Molly as she was my most frequent visitor, or perhaps my mother. But Geoffrey Canfield? I wondered at how he would explain away his wanting to talk to an American partisan, actually two of us. Paul's presence was baffling. Even more incomprehensible was the arrival of my sister.

Molly had been to see us before, bringing food and blankets. However, her appearance with Geoffrey confused me. My mind was swimming with possibilities, most along the lines of our release, but none even came close to what they had come to share.

"What do you mean he's missing?" My ears heard what Geoffrey said, but my mind wasn't comprehending. The idea was unimaginable.

"Molly had asked me to intervene when Henry didn't return from a morning's errand. We scoured the city for him, but so far, he hasn't turned up. We learned some news from . . ."

"Henry just doesn't go off by himself. He . . . he . . ." I shook my head in disgust. "Did you try the wharves? For the past six months or so, he's preoccupied by sailors, ships, and the ocean. Maybe . . ."

"If you're thinking that he's gone aboard a ship for an exploratory adventure, you're mistaken. No sailor would invite an American to board unless he was planning to enlist. And Henry is too smart to think he could sneak onto a ship to simply look around."

My friend was talking in circles and I could feel he was beginning to close in on the truth. In the back of my mind, I feared what he would say. My eyes turned toward Molly, and her face told me all I needed to know. Henry had been impressed. He wouldn't be back.

Geoffrey saw what I knew, but said it aloud for Paul, who was still slightly confused by everything.

"Captain Morgan's men took him. They've been up and down the coast for months kidnapping boys and men."

"But Henry doesn't know anything about sailing!"

"It won't matter, Paul. Morgan needs men to work his smuggling, and with the British closing down illegal operations, he needs a continual supply of replacements."

"Henry could die?"

"I hate to say it, but yes. For the men on board the Hornet, death is a possibility. It will be up to Henry to quickly learn how to survive."

Molly, who had been quiet to this point, approached Paul and me, drawing us into a three-way embrace. We stood there, in silence, contemplating all we had been told and finding comfort in one another's arms.

I felt Geoffrey's hand on my back. "First, we work to get you out of here. Then we go find Henry."

Henry Weston

I couldn't wait to head out of The Three Lions to buy my lottery ticket. My winning lottery ticket! Eli had been good enough to turn away whenever he saw my fingers in the till. It felt good to be out of the tavern and feel the cold breeze on my face. The brisk air refreshed me and the cold temperature added some liveliness to my step. Even the steel gray sky, though it threatened a storm, couldn't dampen my enthusiasm today. My happiness would be shared by everyone once they realized that my bet had paid off and I had generously contributed to the tavern's earnings.

When I stepped out, rather than turning right and heading toward Faneuil Hall, I went left. My friend, Seth Cargill, worked near the Customs House, and I'd said I'd also pick up a ticket for him. Trouble was, I didn't have the money to buy both tickets unless he paid me first.

As I approached the wharf, I could see that there were lots of sailors bustling here and there loading boxes and crates onto one of the ships. When Eli worked at the wharf, I had spent lots of time watching the sailors come and go. The tars, especially those who disembarked from long journeys, always had a tale or two to share with a young boy.

"There you are!"

I heard Seth's tenor voice pierce the hubbub and finally located him standing next to a high stack of crates that was growing steadily smaller as the dockworkers kept on loading.

"Got the money?"

All the sailors, dockworkers, and a few unseemly types milling around made me a bit anxious about exchanging money in such an open place. I breathed deeply and told myself that it would be over quickly enough. I wanted his money in my hand, and my hand in my pocket, so I could leave as soon as possible.

185

"Course I do!" Seth had never been an organized person, and he began to fish in his pockets for the coins. He rummaged through every pocket: left pants pocket, right pants pocket, pockets in his jacket and vest! Time kept ticking by, and more eyes were starting to pay attention to us. With each passing moment, I grew more nervous.

"Hurry up!" I urged my friend.

Suddenly, a large, calloused hand clamped over my outstretched palm, grabbing the money as well as my hand. A second hand wrapped around my mouth silencing my call for help. His body closed in on mine and I could feel his bulk beneath the layers of winter clothes we both wore.

A second sailor had gripped Seth by the arms and manhandled him to the ground. As I struggled against my attacker, a third man placed a burlap corn sack over my friend's head and tied it with a rough length of rope. He stood up and approached us, leaving the second man to pummel Seth on the ground. There was no time to waste if I were to escape, so I bent forward and turned into my attacker's arm. He was more experienced in fighting than I, and he sensed my next move. He bent and turned with me, successfully blocking my escape route. He jerked me upright and a second bag went over my head.

"Put 'em aboard quickly. We sail in an hour."

The voice didn't come from behind me, rather, to my left. It was loud and gravelly, but most of all, authoritative. Could that be the captain? He knew what was going on?

Someone grabbed my hands and bound them together. My feet left the ground and my head upended as the attacker threw me over his shoulder, and I felt another rope winding around my ankles and then pulled taut. The gangway bowed and creaked as my attacker carried me aboard ship. I counted thirty steps and then felt nothing but air followed by a hard landing as I hit the wooden deck. A few kicks to my legs and backside left me writhing in pain.

As soon as I caught my breath, I sought out my friend.

"Seth? Seth!"

A low mumble reassured me that he too had boarded.

We lay there, immobile, for a time. It seemed longer than it probably was for the cold had seeped into our bones and we were shivering uncontrollably by the time we realized the ship was leaving its mooring. Men shouted at one another and we felt their feet pounding up and down the deck. Then we heard a sharp crack as the sails unfurled and the wind caught the canvas. Soon the ship's prow was crashing headlong into the waves, sending plumes of saltwater over the bow and down onto her hostages.

"Seth?"

"Mmm?"

"I don't think we're in Boston anymore."

to be continued . . .

Read on to the first chapter of *Revolutionary Spark*

Revolutionary Spark

February 1768

Molly Weston

"That can't possibly be true!"

"What are you referring to, Molly?"

Mother and I were rolling dough into biscuits, well, mostly she was rolling as I had dusted off my hands to read the Monday advices in the *Gazette*.

"Listen to this:"

> Small common Field Peas, burnt carefully with Butter, and ground as Coffee, has been tryed by several Persons in this Town, and found equal, if not superior, to the Produce of the West Indies. —Quere, How many Thousands may be save annually by this Discovery?[48]"

"Well, it might serve to make a tasty warm drink, but to substitute peas for tea? Ha! I scoff at the very idea!"

"Daughter, whatever makes sense to save a few pennies is worth trying. Let's experiment. Do we have any dried peas left from

---

[48] *Boston-Gazette, and Country Journal*, February 7, 1768.

our summer harvest? Perhaps we could plump them with water and try this receipt."

"I'd rather drink that Labrador concoction!"

Mother clucked her tongue and smiled knowing full well I would never touch that brew — it left such a sour taste in the mouth! Merchants had been gathering herbs from the lake country to fulfill the thirst Bostonians had for tea, but there were rumors that people were becoming ill from drinking the concoction. We both knew that the rumors were being spread by Tory merchants who were selling imports on the side.

Tea was still available from these suppliers, but mother and I were resolute in our abstinence. The Sons of Liberty had reported several merchants moving the crates of tea into their warehouses, claiming they wouldn't sell it. Yet, it seemed that the tea trade flourished within the city. Mother still had friends who had hoarded their own supply of tea for "medicinal" purposes, and even some of the girls in my age group would "visit" their ill friends every afternoon — all a ruse to partake of the beverage our patriots were actively boycotting. Some weeks it seemed as if everyone was ill on a different day, enabling women to tend to their friends on a rotating schedule.

Mother and I were in a happier mood than we had been in for a long time. We finally had Eli and Paul back at home. Geoffrey had been true to his word. The arrest of my brothers in November 1767 along with four other men had shaken our family. They had moved out of the tavern and lived by felling timber in the nearby forests. The Royal Navy was building up its supply of warships to counter the ever-growing Spanish fleet. The tallest and straightest white pine grew in America, and the best were selected for the Crown.

Eli and Paul, along with Eli's best friend Cotton, and a few other men, had begun to stash some of the choicest logs. It was a successful attempt to foil the British from pillaging a valuable resource, until a platoon of British regulars intercepted a missive and raided the logging camp. Although Cotton was able to escape capture, the others were imprisoned.

Mercy Otis Warren, whom I knew from working in a local shop, promised her brother's help to free my brothers. Yet her promise of a quick release was not to be. In short time, my brothers were transferred to Watertown jail, and I began to look for another lawyer who could help. The rants of James Otis in the Assembly and elsewhere were becoming more commonplace, and many people in town were beginning to gossip about his mental capacity. As much as I appreciated all that Mercy was doing on our behalf, I couldn't rely on her brother to be the solicitor we needed.

Father then turned to Samuel Adams for assistance, who in turn asked his relative John Adams to step in. With someone of his stature, we felt sure that the situation would turn around. And it did. The words of the Crown's solicitor were turned back on him by Mr. Adams and, in the end, the loggers went free.

Our mood would have been lighter had our dear Henry also been back in our fold. Impressed in January, we hadn't heard from him, although we checked with every ship for correspondence.

"It's likely he won't be able to write," Geoffrey had cautioned us early on. "They'll be at sea for weeks at a time, and once he is in port, he will be closely watched until the boatswain's sure he won't run. After that, perhaps we'll have word from him."

Mother and I believed in Henry. He had a quick mind and was perceptive to people and his surroundings. He was good with ciphering and was fleet-footed. More than anything, I needed to believe that he would survive life aboard the Hornet Sloop of War and come home to Boston. I refused to believe otherwise.

If you've enjoyed reading *Revolutionary Spirit*, be sure to tell your friends!

Follow the Patriots at *www.loripiotrowski.com* and sign up for my newsletter for information about speaking engagements, book signings, fun facts I find while researching, and upcoming releases!

Addenda

Holiday Cooky
Currency Act of 1764
Declaratory Act of 1766
An Inquiry Into the Rights of the British Colonies
Townshend Revenue Act
References

Addenda

Holiday Cooky

3   cups all-purpose flour
3-4 tbsp. ground coriander (more or less to taste)
1¾ cups sugar
¾   cup cold unsalted butter, diced
¾   tsp. baking soda
1/3 cup plus 3-4 Tbsp. milk, depending on need
American Heritage Chocolate (optional for decorating)

Preheat oven to 325° F.
Grease several cookie sheets.

Stir together flour, sugar, and coriander.
Use a pastry blender to cut butter into flour mixture to reach a coarse meal consistency.

Stir baking soda into 1/3 cup of the milk. Add the milk to the flour-butter mixture and mix. Continue adding milk by tablespoon and knead the mixture until reaching a stiff, smooth dough.

Wrap in wax paper and chill. Divide the dough into halves for rolling out, keeping the unused portion cool.

Sprinkle flour or powdered sugar onto a smooth surface. Roll out dough to 1/3 – ½ inch thickness. Use a cookie cutter or stamp to make the forms.

Transfer the shapes onto the baking sheets, spacing them 1" apart.

Bake for 18-23 minutes, until slightly browned at the edge. Transfer cookies to a cooling rack.

In a double boiler, melt the American Heritage chocolate chunks, stirring to ensure the chocolate melts completely. Use a spoon or knife to dab onto the cooled cookies.

Store the cookies in an airtight container, layering with a sheet of parchment or waxed paper to keep the chocolate from sticking to the cookie on top.

Cookie recipe adapted from Nancy Baggett, *The All-American Cookie Book,* Houghton Mifflin Company: Boston, MA and New York, NY. 2001. American Heritage Chocolate is a product of MARS and may be purchased online at http://www.AmericanHeritageChocolate.com.

Currency Act of 1764

WHEREAS great quantities of paper bills of credit have been created and issued in his Majesty's colonies or plantations in America, by virtue of acts, orders, resolutions, or votes of assembly, making and declaring such bills of credit to be legal tender in payment of money: and whereas such bills of credit have greatly depreciated in their value, by means whereof debts have been discharged with a much less value than was contracted for, to the great discouragement and prejudice of the trade and commerce of his Majesty's subjects, by occasioning confusion in dealings, and lessening credit in the said colonies or plantations: for remedy whereof, may it please your most excellent Majesty, that it may be enacted; and be it enacted by the King's most excellent majesty, by and with the advice and consent of the lords spiritual and temporal, and commons, in this present parliament assembled, and by the authority of the same, That from and after the first day of September, one thousand seven hundred and sixty four, no act, order, resolution, or vote of assembly, in any of his Majesty's colonies or plantations in America, shall be made, for creating or issuing any paper bills, or bills of credit of any kind or denomination whatsoever, declaring such paper bills, or bills of credit, to be legal tender in payment of any bargains, contracts, debts, dues, or demands whatsoever; and every clause or provision which shall hereafter be inserted in any act, order, resolution, or vote of assembly, contrary to this act, shall be null and void.

II. And whereas the great quantities of paper bills, or bills of credit, which are now actually in circulation and currency in several colonies or plantations in America, emitted in pursuance of acts of assembly declaring such bills a legal tender, make it highly expedient that the conditions and terms, upon which such bills have been emitted, should not be varied or prolonged, so as to continue the legal tender thereof beyond the terms respectively fixed by such acts for calling in and discharging such bills; be it therefore enacted by the authority aforesaid, That every act, order, resolution, or vote of assembly, in any of the said colonies or plantations, which shall be made to prolong the legal tender of any paper bills, or bills of credit, which are now subsisting and current in any of the said colonies or plantations in America, beyond the times fixed for the calling in, sinking, and discharging of such paper bills, or bills of credit, shall be null and void.

III. And be it further enacted by the authority aforesaid, That if any governor or commander in chief for the time being, in all or any of the said colonies or plantations, shall, from and after the said first day of September, one thousand seven hundred and sixty four, give his assent to any act or order of assembly contrary to the true intent and meaning of this act, every such governor or commander in chief shall, for every such offence, forfeit and pay the sum of one thousand pounds, and shall be immediately dismissed from his government, and for ever after rendered incapable of any public office or place of trust.

IV. Provided always, That nothing in this act shall extend to alter or repeal an act passed in the twenty fourth year of the reign of his late majesty King George the Second, intituled, An act to regulate and restrain paper bills of credit in his Majesty's colonies or plantations of Rhode Island and Providence plantations, Connecticut, the Massachuset's Bay, and New Hampshire, in America, and to prevent the same being legal tenders in payments of money.

V. Provided also, That nothing herein contained shall extend, or be construed to extend, to make any of the bills now subsisting in any of the said colonies a legal tender.

Declaratory Act of 1766
March 18, 1766

AN ACT for the better securing the dependency of his Majesty's dominions in America upon the crown and parliament of Great Britain.

WHEREAS several of the houses of representatives in his Majesty's colonies and plantations in America, have of late, against law, claimed to themselves, or to the general assemblies of the same, the sole and exclusive right of imposing duties and taxes upon his Majesty's subjects in the said colonies and plantations; and have, in pursuance of such claim, passed certain votes, resolutions, and orders, derogatory to the legislative authority of parliament, and inconsistent with the dependency of the said colonies and plantations upon the crown of Great Britain: ... be it declared ...,

That the said colonies and plantations in *America* have been, are, and of right ought to be. subordinate unto, and dependent upon the imperial crown and parliament of *Great Britain*; and that the King's majesty, by and with the advice and consent of the lords spiritual and temporal, and commons of *Great Britain*, in parliament assembled, had, hath, and of right ought to have, full power and authority to make laws and statutes of sufficient force and validity to bind the colonies and people of *America*, subjects of the crown of *Great Britain*, in all cases whatsoever.

II. And be it further declared ..., That all resolutions, votes, orders, and proceedings, in any of the said colonies or plantations, whereby the power and authority of the parliament of *Great Britain*, to make laws and statutes as aforesaid, is denied, or drawn into question, are, and are hereby declared to be, utterly null and void to all intents and purposes whatsoever.

An Inquiry Into the Rights of the British Colonies
by Richard Bland, 1766

(Written in response to Thomas Whately's 1765 defense of the Stamp Act, of which he was the author.)

The Question is whether the Colonies are represented in the *British* Parliament or not? You affirm it to be indubitable Fact that they are represented, and from thence you infer a Right in the Parliament to impose Taxes of every Kind upon them. You do not insist upon the *Power*, but upon the *Right* of Parliament to impose Taxes upon the Colonies. This is certainly a very proper Distinction, as *Right* and *Power* have very different Meanings, and convey very different Ideas: For had you told us that the Parliament of *Great Britain* have *Power*, by the Fleets and Armies of the Kingdom, to impose Taxes and to raise Contributions upon the Colonies, I should not have to presumed to dispute the Point with you; but as you insist upon the *Right* only, I must beg Leave to differ from you in Opinion, and shall give my Reasons for it.

* * * *

I cannot comprehend how Men who are excluded from voting at the Election of Members of Parliament can be represented in that Assembly, or how those who are elected do not sit in the House as Representatives of their Constituents. These Assertions appear to me not only paradoxical, but contrary to the fundamental Principles of the *English* Constitution.

To illustrate this important Disquisition, I conceive we must recur to the civil Constitution of *England,* and from thence deduce and ascertain the Rights and Privileges of the People at the first Establishment of the Government, and discover the Alterations that

199

have been made in them from Time to Time; and it is from the Laws of the Kingdom, founded upon the Principles of the Law of Nature, that we are to show the Obligation every Member of the State is under to pay Obedience to its Institutions. From these Principles I shall endeavor to prove that the Inhabitants of *Britain*, who have no Vote in the Election of Members of Parliament, are not represented in that Assembly, and yet that they owe Obedience to the Laws of Parliament; which, as to them, are constitutional, and not arbitrary. As to the Colonies, I shall consider them afterwards.

Now it is a Fact, as certain as History can make it, that the present civil Constitution of *England* derives its Original from those *Saxons* who, coming over to the Assistance of the *Britons* in the Time of their King *Vortiger* made themselves Masters of the Kingdom, and established a Form of Government in it similar to that they had been accustomed to live under in their native Country as similar, at least, as the Difference of their Situation and Circumstances would permit. This Government, like that from whence they came, was founded upon Principles of the most perfect Liberty: The conquered Lands were divided among the Individuals in Proportion to the Rank they held in the Nation, and every Freeman, that is, every Freeholder, was a member of their Wittinagemot, or Parliament. The other Part of the Nation, or the Non-Proprietors of Land, were of little Estimation. They, as in *Germany*, were either Slaves, mere Hewers of Wood and Drawers of Water, or Freedmen; who, being of foreign Extraction, had been manumitted by their Masters, and were excluded from the high Privilege of having a Share in the Administration of the Commonwealth, unless they became Proprietors of Land (which they might obtain by Purchase or Donation) and in that Case they has a Right to sit with the Freemen, in the Parliament or sovereign Legislature of the State.

How long this Right of being personally present in the Parliament continued, or when the Custom of sending Representatives to this great Council of the Nation, was first introduced, cannot be determined with Precision; but let the Custom of Representation be introduced when it will, it is certain that every Freeman, or, which was the same Thing in the Eye of the Constitution, every Freeholder, had a right to vote at the Election of Members of Parliament, and therefore might be said, with great Propriety, to be present in that Assembly, either in his own Person or by Representation. This Right of Election in the Freeholders is evident from the Statute 1st Hen. 5. Ch. 1st, which limits the Right of Election to those Freeholders only who are resident in the Counties the Day of the Date of the Writ of Election; but yet every resident Freeholder indiscriminately, let his Freehold be ever so small, had a Right to vote at the Election of Knights for his County so that they were actually represented. And this Right of Election continued until it was taken away by the Statute 8th Hen. 6 Ch. 7. Shillings by the year at the least.

Now this statute was deprivative of the Right of those Freeholders who came within the Description of it; but of what did it deprive them, if they were represented notwithstanding their Right of Election was taken from them? The mere Act of voting was nothing, of no Value, if they were represented as constitutionally without it as with it: But when by the fundamental Principles of the Constitution they were to be considered as Members of the Legislature, and as such had a right to be present in Person, or to send their Procurators or Attornies, and by them to give their Suffrage in the supreme Council of the Nation, this Statute deprived them of an essential Right; a Right without which by the ancient Constitution of the State, all other Liberties were but a Species of Bondage.

As these Freeholders then were deprived of their Rights to substitute Delegates to Parliament, they could not be represented, but were placed in the same Condition with the Non-Proprietors of Land, who were excluded by the original Constitution from having any Share in the Legislature, but who, notwithstanding such Exclusion, are bound to pay Obedience to the Laws of Parliament, even if they should consist of nine Tenths of the People of *Britain*; but then the Obligation of these Laws does not arise from their being virtually represented in Parliament, but from a quite different Reason.

* * * *

From hence it is evident that the Obligation of the Laws of Parliament upon the People of *Britain* who have no Right to be Electors does not arise from their being *virtually* represented, but from a quit different Principle; a Principle of the Law of Nature, true, certain, and universal, applicable to every Sort of Government, and not contrary to the common Understandings of Mankind.

If what you say is real Fact, that the nine Tenths of the People of *Britain* are deprived of the high Privilege of being Electors, it shows a great Defect in the present Constitution, which has departed so much from its original Purity; but never can prove that those People are even *virtually* represented in Parliament. And here give me Leave to observe that it would be a Work worthy of the best patriotick Spirits in the Nation to effectuate an Alteration in this putrid Part of the Constitution; and, by restoring it to its pristine Perfection, prevent any "Order or Rank of the Subjects from imposing upon or binding the rest without their Consent." But, I fear, the Gangrene has taken too deep Hold to be eradicated in these Days of Venality.

But if those People of *Britain* who are excluded from being Electors are not represented in Parliament, the Conclusion is much stronger against the People of the Colonies being represented; who are considered by the *British* Government itself, in every Instance of Parliamentary Legislation, as a distinct People.

* * * *

As then we can receive no Light from the Laws of the Kingdom, or from ancient History, to direct us in out Inquiry, we must have Recourse to the Law of Nature, and those Rights of Mankind which flow from it.

I have observed before that when Subjects are deprived of their civil Rights, or are dissatisfied with the Place they hold in the Community, they have a natural Right to quit the Society of which they are Members, and to retire into another Country. Now when Men exercise this Right, and withdraw themselves from their Country, they recover their natural Freedom and Independence: The Jurisdiction and Sovereignty of the State they have quitted ceases; and if they unite, and by common Consent take Possession of a New Country, and form themselves into a political Society, they become a sovereign State, independent of the State from which they have separated. If then the Subjects of *England* have a natural Right to relinquish their Country, and by retiring from it, and associating together, to form a new political Society and independent State, they must have a Right, by Compact with Sovereign of the Nation, to remove into a new Country, and to form a civil Establishment upon the Terms of the Compact. In such a Case, the Terms of the Compact must be obligatory and binding upon the Parties; they must be the Magna Charta, the fundamental Principles of Government, to this new Society; and every Infringement of them must be wrong, and may be opposed. It will be necessary then to examine whether any such Compact was entered into between the Sovereign and those *English* Subjects who established themselves in *America*.

The Townshend Revenue Act
June 29, 1767

AN ACT for granting certain duties in the British *colonies and plantations in* America; *for allowing a drawback of the duties of customs upon the exportation from this kingdom, of coffee and cocoa nuts of the produce of the said colonies or plantations; for discontinuing the drawbacks payable on china earthen ware exported to America; and for more effectually preventing the clandestine running of goods in the said colonies and plantations.*

WHEREAS it is expedient that a revenue should be raised, in your Majesty's dominions in America, *for making a more certain and adequate provision for defraying the charge of the administration of justice, and the support of civil government, in such provinces as it shall be found necessary; and towards further defraying the expenses of defending, protecting and securing the said dominions;* ... be it enacted.... That from and after the twentieth day of November, one thousand seven hundred and sixty seven, there shall be raised, levied, collected, and paid, unto his Majesty, his heirs, and successors, for upon and the respective Goods here in after mentioned, which shall be imported from *Great Britain* into any colony or plantation in *America* which now is or hereafter may be, under the dominion of his Majesty, his heirs, or successors, the several Rates and Duties following; that is to say,

For every hundredweight avoirdupois of crown, plate, flint, and white glass, four shillings and eight pence.
For every hundred weight avoirdupois of red lead, two shillings.
For every hundred weight avoirdupois of green glass, one shilling and two pence.
For every hundred weight avoirdupois of white lead, two shillings.
For every hundred weight avoirdupois of painters colours, two shillings.

For every pound weight avoirdupois of tea, three pence.

For every ream of paper, usually called or known by the name of *Atlas fine*, twelve shillings. ...

IV

...and that all the monies that shall arise by the said duties (except the necessary charges of raising, collecting, levying, recovering, answering, paying, and accounting for the same) shall be applied, in the first place, in such manner as is herein after mentioned, in making a more certain and adequate provision for the charge of the administration of justice, and the support of civil government in such of the said colonies and plantations where it shall be found necessary; and that the residue of such duties shall be payed into the receipt of his Majesty's exchequer, and shall be entered separate and apart from all other monies paid or payable to his Majesty ...; and shall be there reserved, to be from time to time disposed of by parliament towards defraying the necessary expense of defending, protecting, and securing, the *British* colonies and plantations in *America*.

V

And be it further enacted ..., That his Majesty and his successors shall be, and are hereby, impowered, from time to time, by any warrant or warrants under his or their royal sign manual or sign manuals, countersigned by the high treasurer, or any three or more of the commissioners of the treasury for the time being, to cause such monies to be applied, out of the produce of the duties granted by this act, as his Majesty, or his successors, shall think proper or necessary, for defraying the charges of the administration of justice, and the support of the civil government, within all or any of the said colonies or plantations....

X

And whereas by an act of parliament made in the fourteenth year of the reign of King Charles the Second, intituled, *An act for preventing frauds, and regulating abuses, in his Majesty's customs,* and several other acts now in force, it is lawful for any officer of his Majesty's customs, authorized by writ of assistance under the seal of his Majesty's court of exchequer, to take a constable, headborough, or other public officer inhabiting near unto the place, and in the daytime to enter and go into any house, shop cellar, warehouse, or room or other place and, in case of resistance, to break open doors, chests, trunks, and other pakage there, to seize, and from thence to bring, any kind of goods or merchandise whatsoever prohibited or uncustomed, and to put and secure the same in his Majesty's storehouse next to the place where such seizure shall be made; and whereas by an act made in the seventh and eighth years of the reign of King William the Third, intituled *An act for preventing frauds, and regulating abuses, in the plantation trade,* it is, amongst other things, enacted, that the officers for collecting and managing his Majesty's revenue, and inspecting the plantation trade, in *America,* shall have the same powers and authorities to enter houses or warehouses, to search or seize goods prohibited to be imported or exported into or out of any of the said plantations, or for which any duties are payable, or ought to have been paid; and that the like assistance shall be given to the said officers in the execution of their office, as, by the said recited act of the fourteenth year of King Charles the Second, is provided for the officers of England: but, no authority being expressly given by the said act, made in the seventh and eighth years of the reign of King William the Third, to any particular court to grant such writs of assistance for the officers of the customs in the said plantations, it is doubted whether such officers can legally enter houses and other places on land, to search for and seize goods, in the manner directed by the said recited acts: To obviate which doubts for the future, and in order to carry the intention of the said recited acts into effectual execution, be it enacted ..., That from and after the said twentieth day of November, one thousand seven hundred and sixty seven, such writs of assistance, to authorize and impower the officers of his Majesty's customs to enter and go into any house, warehouse, shop, cellar, or other place, in the *British* colonies or plantations in *America,* to search for and seize prohibited and uncustomed goods, in the manner directed by the said recited acts, shall and may be granted by the said superior or supreme court of justice having jurisdiction within such colony or plantation respectively...

References

Adair, D. and Schutz, J.A. (Eds.). (1961). *Peter Oliver's Origin & Progress of the American Rebellion: A Tory View*. San Marino, CA: The Huntington Library.

Baggett, N. (2001). *The All-American cookie book. Boston, MA and New York, NY: Houghton Mifflin Company*.

Carp. B. L. (2007). *Rebels rising: Cities and the American Revolution*. New York, NY: Oxford University Press.

Klepp, S. E. and Wulf, K. (Eds.). (2010). *The diary of Hannah Callendar Sanson: Sense and sensibility in the age of the American Revolution*. Ithaca, NY and London, Great Britain: Cornell University Press.

Knollenberg, Bernhard. (1975). Growth of the American Revolution 1766-1775. The Free Press, a division of Macmillan Publishing Co., Inc.: New York, NY.

Nash, G. B. (2005). *The unknown American Revolution: The unruly birth of democracy and the struggle to create America*. New York: NY: Viking Penguin.

Northeastern Lumber Manufacturers Association. http://www.nelma.org.

The Stamp Act History. http://www.stamp-act-history.com

98072346R00133

Made in the USA
Columbia, SC
19 June 2018